Along the Way

A novel

KELSEY LASHER

Along the Way

Chapter 1

THE APPLAUSE WAS DEAFENING. DEAFENING BUT NOT unwelcome. It was one of Ellie's favorite sounds, second only to music. Not because it made her feel good about herself or even because it assured her that she had done her job well. No, Ellie Baxter loved the sound of applause because it made her feel known and understood. Like the sound waves, she had sent forth had done their powerful and predicable work of explaining and defining her to those that listened.

Ellie smiled and sighed in contentment as she walked off the stage, violin and bow in hand, along with the rest of the members of the Seattle Symphony Orchestra. She recognized the same look of contentment in their faces as well.

"That's an item checked off the bucket list for sure," a member of the percussion section said behind her. "Can you believe we got to play with Trace Jones?"

"I've been pinching myself all night!" Someone else said.

Ellie didn't reply, but she agreed with every word. They had been invited to accompany Grammy award winner Trace Jones for a portion of his sold-out concert in Seattle that night, and everyone was relishing the moment.

Ellie followed the rest of the musicians into the dark hallway that led to the green room, the smell of fog from the light show hanging heavy in the air. Ellie usually preferred fresh air, but just for tonight, she relished the sweet, burnt fragrance. It smelled like the electricity, the drama, the adrenaline that only performing could provide, and she loved it. She didn't want a single one of her senses excluded from the moment. Not in the least.

The hallway of the arena stretched out before them, lit dimly by fluorescent lights buzzing above. It was a far cry from Benaroya Hall where they usually performed. It lacked elegance and beauty, but they had more than supplied that with the music they had created.

She would never forget how good it had felt. How transcendent. She would not soon forget how she felt while the music flowed through every inch of her, through every inch of everyone in the arena. To be permeated by sound with thousands of people, to be one of the lucky ones creating that sound… it must have been close to how God had felt as he gazed out on creation.

I made this. I love this. I am found within this, She had thought.

She sighed in contentment, allowing the concrete floor to lead her feet.

"Are you happy, Elle?" her friend and roommate Sarah asked, looping her arm through Ellie's.

"The happiest," Ellie replied softly through a smile, gladly walking the length of the hall with Sarah. "There isn't anyone else I would rather share this with, either."

Sarah smiled and squeezed Ellie's hand in response, and Ellie knew she agreed. Although they had only been friends for a short eighteen months, each knew the other inside and out. Perhaps it was because they had both found themselves alone in a new city, desperate for a friend. Perhaps it was their shared love for music and baked goods. Whatever the reason, Ellie had meant what she said. Sarah was her best friend and, aside from those she loved back home, the only person she wanted to share such an experience with.

The two friends made their way through the double doors that opened up into the green room. It was a large, ambiguous space, littered with instrument cases, garment bags, backpacks, and sheet music. On the far, battered wall stood a table heavy with champagne and glasses. A card from Trace Jones thanking them for the collaboration sat in the middle, waiting to travel around the room along with the bubbly beverage.

Ellie and Sarah watched, laughing as a few people popped open the champagne and everyone cheered in response.

"I'll go get us a glass!" Sarah yelled over the noise. "You wait here."

Ellie watched as Sarah weaved her way through the crowd, smiling and chatting as she went.

"Aren't you going to get something to drink?" A voice cut through the celebratory buzz behind her. It held a deep timbre and was marked by a faint southern drawl. The sound lulled and soothed her, drew her in, and tugged on her senses like sleep or a lullaby.

"My friend is getting it…" Ellie said with a smile as she turned to reply. The words died on her lips, and she was suddenly speechless. And, judging by the heat that filled her face, probably blushing too.

"Trace Jones!" She blurted out when she finally came to her senses. "You're Trace Jones!"

The man laughed, a deep sound that managed to be melodic and raspy at the same time. "I am! And you're Ellie right?"

"How do you know my name?" She said, eyes wide.

"I asked around," he shrugged. "I hope that's alright."

"Of course! I mean, this is your show, you have every right to know the names of those you invite on stage with you. I just didn't think you would care. Especially not about one little violinist."

"Well," he smiled, "I do."

Ellie blushed further and tried to look away from him, but his blue eyes were too enchanting and extremely kind. In preparation for this show, she had read every interview he had done recently and there were many due to his platinum record that was released a few months before. She thought that he came across as humble and kind but had assumed it was an act, a persona to sell as many records and concert tickets as possible. Never in her wildest dreams did she think he actually possessed those traits!

Unless maybe he wasn't being kind. Maybe she had done something wrong, played the wrong note, the wrong dynamic, the wrong something, and he was seeking her out to address it. Perhaps she had embarrassed him. She had to apologize right away!

"Mr. Jones, I'm sorry if I did something wrong on stage. Hopefully, no one noticed!" Ellie mumbled. "You were phenomenal, you're always phenomenal, and I hate to think that I ruined your show."

He scowled and leaned back in confusion as he tilted his head to the side. "Ellie, what are you talking about? You did nothing wrong! You were spectacular! Mesmerizing! Too mesmerizing. I haven't been able to take my eyes off of you, especially while you're playing."

He laughed softly, shoved his hands in his jean pockets, cocked his head to the side, and smiled.

"Oh… well, I just assumed the only reason you would seek me out was that I had done something wrong. Why else would you ask someone what my name was and approach me?"

She was rambling. A telltale sign that she was flustered.

"Well, I asked around about you because I wanted to know your name and if you're dating anyone. I thought it was safer than risking rejection. Even rock stars like me don't enjoy that," he added with a charming shrug and smile.

"Rejection…? You mean, you're asking me out? You! You are asking me out?" Ellie blurted. She couldn't imagine how very red she was by now, but there was nothing to be done about it.

"I'm trying to," Trace said still smiling. "And I would very much like it if you said yes, Ellie Baxter, the masterful violinist from Colorado."

"You really did ask around," Ellie replied softly.

He nodded, hands still in his pocket, blue eyes still holding hers. The noise level in the room hadn't died down in the least, but Ellie no longer noticed it, no longer noticed the laughter and cheers and bright lighting. This moment felt far too surreal for such ordinary sounds and sights.

Ellie narrowed her eyes and smiled back at him. "I bet you do this all the time, don't you? Ask women out."

"I actually don't. Hardly ever. My mother raised me to be a one-woman man, but life on the road isn't very conducive to relationships. I tend to avoid dating while I'm on tour, but you're too extraordinary to miss out on."

"How do I know you're being honest with me?"

He crossed his arms and tilted his head in thought. "How about this? How about you give me your number and I give you mine. That way, this whole thing will be resting in both of our hands. I promise not to leave you sitting around waiting for my call, as long as you don't leave me sitting around waiting either." He winked at her and she couldn't help but laugh in return.

Why not? She wasn't dating anyone else. What did she have to lose?

Your heart. Again. Just like every other time, Her mind chided. She forced the dark thoughts away, though. Sure, she had only ever known heartbreak in love, but Trace seemed genuinely kind, they shared a love for music, and of course, he was gorgeous in a rugged kind of way. She had to force herself to take the risk.

"Deal," she finally said. "I just need to go and get my phone out of my bag over there. Why don't you walk with me and I'll give you my number on the way."

They weaved their way through pockets of people all with glasses in hand until they reached the chair in the corner where Ellie's purse sat. Trace smiled as they went, shaking hands and offering his thanks to every single person they passed. When they finally made it across the room, he slid his hand onto the small of Ellie's back and leaned in close to her ear.

"Amid my nerves about asking you out, I forgot to thank you. That performance was spectacular. One I'll never forget!"

"It's you I should be thanking, Trace! You gave us all a memory to last a lifetime!"

He smiled at her and, they stood there for the briefest of moments, holding an anticipatory buzz between them. Ellie couldn't stop the hope from rising within her. This was quickly becoming one of the most memorable nights of her life.

"Are you sure about this?" Ellie teased as she fished her phone out of her brown leather purse. "It's not too late to back out, take my number and leave me on the hook for however long you want."

"You wound me, Ms. Baxter! I see I have a lot of work to do in breaking down your misconceptions about us musicians."

Ellie laughed. "I look forward to that."

There. She could flirt a little. And she hadn't even had any champagne yet!

"Found it!" Ellie exclaimed, finally pulling her phone out of her bag. "Oh, wow! I have a million notifications."

"Popular, I see."

"No, it's just from everyone back home in Colorado. My family and our neighbors, who are as good as family, all text all day. I must have missed something."

"Is everything ok?" Trace said, genuine concern lacing his tone.

"I don't know…" Ellie said as she scrolled through everything. She knew she sounded distracted but she had six missed calls from her mom and a few voicemails to match. "It's just that my mom called me six times and she knew I was on stage. She doesn't usually call during shows…"

"Well, why don't you call her back. Mothers should not be kept waiting. I'll sit right here and guard your purse," Trace said gesturing towards the seat beside him. He sat down and stretched, comfortable in the moment.

"Ok, it'll be quick," Ellie said already dialing her mom's number. `

She answered after only one ring.

"Mom? Hi! I saw you called. Is everything ok?" Ellie said still looking at Trace and smiling. Sarah had found her by now. She handed Ellie a sparkling glass of champagne with a question in her eye as she looked from Ellie to Trace.

"Ellie, honey, no everything is not ok," her mother replied. Ellie heard tears in her voice, heard how thin and hollow it sounded. Ellie's smile fell instantly, and her stomach plummeted. Everything in the room suddenly began to move in slow motion. Trace's blue eyes dimmed to a dull gleam. The smell of champagne turned rancid in her nostrils, and all she heard were her mother's words and the buzzing of the fluorescent lights above her.

"It's your brother Cully," her mother said on a sob. "There's been an accident."

* * *

Sutton Pierce sat quietly at the end of the bar, waiting for enough time to pass before he could politely take his leave from the office happy hour celebration. It wasn't that he didn't enjoy this kind of thing. He usually did. Especially when it was to celebrate a case that he had personally won. But tonight was different.

He took another sip of his Old Fashioned and swirled the glass between his fingers as he listened half-heartedly to the conversation surrounding him.

"She objected, but there was no way Sutton was going to let it slide, were you Pierce? Not after everything that happened between you two," His co-council, Mark Jacobson, said.

Sutton didn't reply, just took another long sip of his drink and offered a nod. He didn't want to talk about this. Not today.

"What do you mean? What happened outside the courtroom?" Came a voice from behind Jacobson. It belonged to one of the interns that had just started a week ago. Sutton didn't answer. He was in no mood for his personal life to be pulled out and examined by strangers over drinks. Jacobson had other ideas, though.

"Oh, the defense attorney is Sutton's ex," he offered a little too loudly. He was on his second cocktail and never could hold his liquor.

"The blonde one?" The intern asked with a suggestive lift of his eyebrows.

"That's the one," Jacobson replied with a smirk.

Sutton hunched over the bar, refusing to acknowledge the line of the conversation. Yes, Kate was beautiful. She could make every eyebrow in the room rise in admiration. His certainly had. He had nearly fallen all over himself to get to her after their first showdown in court four years before. He couldn't ask her out fast enough, couldn't kiss her fast enough, couldn't fall in love with her fast enough. But that was all in the past now. Exactly where she wanted it to be.

"Based on how she nearly bulldozed anyone who so much as looked at her in that courtroom, I bet she was the type of woman who would chew you up and spit you out, Mr. Pierce," the intern said sympathetically.

"That's exactly the type of woman she is," Sutton replied pointedly.

"So you went in guns blazing this week and flattened her client," Jacobson cut in raising his glass in salute.

Sutton smiled and shrugged. It had felt good to beat Kate, had felt delicious in an evil sort of way to strip down her argument and leave her bare and defenseless in front of the jury. She had broken his heart, after all. Destroyed the future he had envisioned for them. So, when he saw that she was defending the client that had defrauded his, he wasn't about to let anything go. She had crushed him personally, but today if only for a moment, he had crushed her professionally.

But, winning or not, seeing Kate had taken its toll.

Sutton finished off his Old Fashioned and slid the glass away. The din of discussion rose around him, filling his ears like cotton, lulling his senses until everything was indistinguishable. That was fine. He was exhausted and didn't have the energy to engage in small talk.

Sutton looked down at his watch. It was only six o'clock. Too early to leave. What he wouldn't give to be outside of these walls, though. To be where he truly wanted to be at that moment.

Rock climbing, camping, laughing with Cully.

Sutton shook his head, still regretting not going with his brother-in-law on their annual climbing trip. Well, annual was probably not the best word for it. Not anymore.

For years, that's what it had been. But over the last few, Sutton had missed it, making excuses about work or Kate. By the time September rolled around each year, he had ended up punting, putting it off until the next fall.

He had thought that this year, he would finally go. He had even told Cully so. But then, the chance to defeat Kate in court had come up, and his battered and vengeful heart hadn't been able to turn down the chance to win. Just one more time.

He hadn't regretted his choice at the time, especially after Cully had given his resounding endorsement of the plan to trounce Kate in court.

"Stay in Portland and show her what she missed out on, Sutton," Cully had said. "I'll call you when I get back to hear all about it."

Sutton could still hear the assurance in Cully's voice, could still hear the music playing in the background of the phone call and his sister Rose's voice offering her support. He couldn't wait to tell Cully that he had done just what he had set out to do, that he hadn't missed their trip in vain.

Yes, it had seemed like a good excuse at the time, but now that it was over, Sutton wished he could somehow make his way back home to Colorado. To the campfire that Cully was inevitably sitting next to right now.

Next year. There would always be next year.

Sutton stood up, intent on stretching his legs and doing his best to mingle with his co-workers. He needed to thank everyone that had helped with the case, needed to shake their hands, and make sure they knew how important their work was. After that, he would sneak out.

Sutton began fighting his way through the crowd towards the group of interns that had assisted him, but his phone buzzing in his pocket stopped him.

"Hey, Mom," he answered loudly over the cacophony of music and voices in the bar. "Can I call you back later? I'm at a work thing."

"Sutton, honey, you can't call me back later. I need to talk to you right now and you need to hear every word I say," his mother replied. Her voice was firm, more firm than he had heard her in a long time. She was usually easy-going, the life of the party, never one to ask anyone to leave a social setting for a phone call. The fact that she was made Sutton's heart beat faster.

"Ok, Mom," he said slowly. "I'm stepping outside. Wait just a minute."

Sutton turned and walked out of the front door. It was raining outside, and his eyes focused on the reflection of the street lights in the puddles the pavement. He pulled his suit jacket closer around him and cked under an awning in an effort to stay dry.

ght, I can hear you now, Mom. What's going on?"

e sighed heavily. "I don't know how to tell you this, Sutton. I ss I just have to say it. It's Cully. He fell. While he was climbing nd, and he's gone… our Cully, gone."

His mother's words swirled in his mind, unable to find a foothold. "What do you mean gone, Mom?"

"I mean, he died, Sutton. They say it was immediate, that he was gone on impact which is a small mercy. I still don't know what we're going to do without him, though," his mother said through tears. Her voice cracked and broke, and Sutton's heart did the same.

His brother-in-law, gone. His best friend, gone.

"No. That can't be right. I should have been there with him, mom," Sutton finally said in a strangled tone. His tie felt like a noose around his neck, but he couldn't bring himself to lift his hands and loosen it. They felt like they were made of concrete, like a thousand pounds of sadness weighed them down.

"No, Sutton, you shouldn't have. You should be right where you are, working hard, doing your job," his mother replied, but her words were no solace to him.

Nothing was.

Sutton went silent, and his mother didn't press him for words. She must have been just as lost in her own grief. He knew how much she loved Cully. She had watched him grow up right alongside her children, had loved him and his brother and sister as her own just like Cully's parents had done for Sutton and his sisters.

Their two families had grown up in lockstep. When Rose and Cully had married five years earlier, solidifying the bond that had always existed between them all, it had only felt right. Had felt like it was about time.

Now, though, it was shattered. Everything was shattered, and Sutton didn't know what to do.

"Sutton," his mother finally said.

"I'm here," he answered in a whisper.

"We want you and Jake and Ellie to come home together. We don't want any of you to be alone at a time like this. Can you do that?"

Jake and Ellie. Cully's brother and sister. They had migrated to the Pacific Northwest like Sutton and were only a few hours away. Despite the lack of distance, Sutton hadn't seen them in almost two years. He hadn't been home in almost two years.

Now, their families wanted them to come home together. Come home so they could bury Cully. The thought made Sutton physically sick, but he would do it. Of course, he would do it. The very thought of seeing Ellie and Jake was a balm to his bruised and beaten heart.

"Sure, mom. We'll be there soon. Tell Rose we're coming."

He hung up the phone, still in shock. All he could do was stare at the puddles, the pools of water holding the light. Cully was gone. All that was left of him was a memory, a mere reflection of the light that he was.

Sutton, still in shock, looked through the window behind him at the scene he had just left. He saw Jacobson laughing with another lawyer, saw his assistant cozy up to one of the interns, saw the partner's arms crossed, eyebrows furrowed, talking business.

This is what he had chosen. These people. This life. This celebration.

This is what he had chosen over Cully. Over the rest of the family. He had pushed them all away in pursuit of the mirage in the window, and now? Well, now there was no next year.

Sutton had to move, had to walk away from the picture he saw. He couldn't look at it without gagging. Regret was choking him.

Grief was strangling him, and he had to move for fear of collapsing on the pavement.

So, he did. He walked aimlessly down the streets of Portland, replaying the last years of his life. Heartache and regret hit him in waves, pushing him farther and farther out onto the seas of grief and confusion.

Sutton lost all track of time and place, but eventually, he stopped and looked up across the street. He didn't know what neighborhood he was in. It was certainly not as upscale as the one he had left. It was comfortable, though. Older buildings lined the street, their windows glowing with light. Groups of people milled around on the sidewalk every few feet, happily chatting or walking together. Sutton looked around until his eyes landed on a bungalow across the street.

It was a small craftsman, painted an eclectic mix of colors. The front door had a peace sign painted on it, and a plastic flamingo rested in the lawn with a cigar hanging from his beak and a pirate's eye patch over its left eye. Sutton chuckled at it and wondered if the owners were looking out at him in his three-piece suit and nice shoes with the same reaction.

To each his own, Sutton thought to himself as he turned to keep walking. As he took another step, though, his eyes snagged on something in the driveway.

A rundown, ugly camper van beckoned him with its still, silent silhouette, and Sutton obeyed. It looked to be a relic from the 1970s, and Sutton grimaced at the rust and wear he felt under his palm as he ran his hand along the door. Cully had talked about buying one just like this when they were teenagers, had wanted to pool their money and fix it up so they could spend summers home from college camping in the Rocky Mountains together.

They had never done it, though, had never made those memories.

Sutton's heart fell for the hundredth time that night, plummeted at the moments they would never have.

Cully would have loved the ugly thing, and Sutton felt that he owed it to his memory to at least admire it, study its details, and dream about the adventures it could hold. So, Sutton circled the van slowly, taking in every last detail until he got to the front.

He froze as his eyes took in what he saw. A "For Sale" sign hung from the windshield, taped just below a crack that stretched from end to end.

Sutton's heart skipped a beat. He could buy it! Buy it and drive himself, Ellie, and Jake home. They could take this ugly, beaten down thing and honor Cully one last time. Feel his memory linger close as they drove home to say goodbye.

Sutton took the front steps in one leap and knocked on the door until someone opened it.

"How much for the camper van?" he asked enthusiastically

Chapter 2

THE SCENT OF ROSES WOKE ELLIE THE NEXT MORNING, heady and beautiful, their fragrance lifting her eyelids like the pulls on window coverings. Ellie's tired eyes opened and landed on two dozen white and red roses sitting on her nightstand. A small note rested against the large vase.

Beautiful Ellie,

I'm so sorry for your loss. I wish you and your family every comfort during this time. I'm only a phone call away if you need anything.

Trace

In an instant, it all came rushing back to her. The whirlwind of emotion that the night before had held. The elation of the concert, the joy of Trace's attention, it had carried her up flight after flight of happiness. An elevator of joy ascending ever higher.

And then it had all come plummeting down.

She remembered how her mother's voice had fallen into her ears like ice water, chilling, shocking, unwanted. Ellie had dropped her glass of champagne and sat absentmindedly on a chair. Trace and Sarah had immediately crowded around her, questioning her about the blank expression on her face.

Ellie hadn't even had the presence of mind to respond to her mother. She said nothing, simply sat there staring at the spot on the carpet where her champagne had landed. She watched as the celebration leaked, watched as the joy that the glass held was absorbed by the floor.

"Ellie, honey, are you there? Ellie…" Her mother's voice rang through the speaker, but still, Ellie said nothing, did nothing. Sarah, eyes full of concern and fear, grabbed Ellie's phone from her hands and immediately placed it to her ear.

"Lisa, it's Sarah. What's wrong?"

Ellie couldn't hear her mother's words, but she felt them. She felt Sarah take the blow, saw Sarah take the blow as her eyes filled with shock and tears. Sarah placed a hand to her stomach as if she would be sick, but she didn't move, just held Ellie's gaze.

"Oh, Lisa, no. I'm so sorry…No, she's just shocked… Yes, I'll get her home. Call you soon."

Ellie hadn't noticed Trace taking her hand. She hadn't noticed how he had stroked the top of it with care and concern. He and Sarah had collected her things and walked her to the car, speaking in hushed tones to each other. Trace had gently helped her into the passenger seat, closed her door, and stood, hands in his pockets as they drove away. Sarah had held her hand the whole drive home. Ellie didn't say a word.

Now, in her bedroom with dull morning light seeping in through her window, she forced herself to come to terms with "her loss," as Trace had put it.

She had lost her oldest brother. Her shining light. The north star of joy for all those she loved.

Ellie climbed out of bed, walked to her window, and opened it to the September air beyond its panes. It was cold and heavy yet comforting. The leaves glowed like they only can in autumn. Somehow, every year the world knew to coat itself in gold. The light, the leaves, the feelings. Golden. Ellie loved it and took a deep breath that smelled of leaves and apples. The sky was grey, the colors muted, the air chilled. It was a melancholy morning, and it suited her.

She closed her eyes, trying to steady her breathing. Ellie looked away from the picture of her brother's face in her mind, and she silenced the sound of his laughter that was ringing within her memories.

Ellie tried to forget how it felt to jump into a crunchy pile of leaves with him, hands intertwined. She fought nausea rising within her, forced a sob to die in her throat.

She felt like she was spinning out of control. Ellie hated that most of all. The grief and devastation she could handle, but the feeling of losing control of her whole world was too much. Precious things were meant to stay. Family was meant to last. They couldn't fall away like leaves on a tree.

So why did she feel like she was? Like she was twirling and tumbling, a leaf withered and dead, cut off from its roots.

A knock came on her bedroom door, rescuing Ellie from the fall she was taking.

"Come in," she answered without turning around. She knew it was Sarah. No one else lived with them.

"I brought you some coffee, Elle," Sarah said gently, as she extended a steaming mug towards her. "It's freezing in here. Why do you have the window open?"

Ellie just shrugged and took the mug from Sarah with a word of thanks. Sarah sat on the bed and wrapped herself in Ellie's down comforter.

"Come sit with me," She said.

Ellie set her mug on the nightstand and sat down beside her friend. Sarah draped the blanket over Ellie's shoulders, and Ellie rested her head on her friend's shoulder. She sighed. Ellie did the same.

"Those flowers are gorgeous. I hope you don't mind that I snuck them into your room this morning. Trace had them sent over earlier, and I wanted you to wake up to them. He seems too good to be true."

"He does, doesn't he? I'm sure that's the last I'll hear from him, though," Ellie said on a yawn.

"Why would you say that?" Sarah asked.

"Because he can have any woman he wants. Why would he stick

around for this mess? It doesn't matter. I can't think about him right now. I can only think about Cully."

A lump rose in Ellie's throat as she said her brother's name. She reached for her coffee, took a gigantic gulp, and forced the lump deep down within her.

"I need to call my parents. I need to call Rose. I need to…"

"I already talked to your mom this morning," Sarah interrupted. "She said everyone is holding up ok but to call when you're ready. Of course, she's worried about you."

"Did she say how Rose is doing?"

"No, but I imagine she's a mess. I would be if my husband died…"

Sarah was cut off by the sound of Ellie's phone ringing. Ellie picked it up and looked at the caller ID.

"It's Sutton," Ellie told Sarah. "I should take this. Hello?"

"Hey Elle," Sutton said. His voice sounded like home, and Ellie's eyes filled with tears as soon as she heard the deep, comforting sound. Sutton's family had lived next door to hers nearly their whole lives. They had grown up as close as siblings, and he was one of her oldest friends.

Ellie hadn't seen him in almost two years and hadn't talked to him since the family video chat last Easter. Not because she hadn't wanted to. Of course, she had, but she understood Sutton's lack of time and freedom. He had moved to Portland a few years ago. Embarking upon a promising and rigorous law career all while enduring a serious relationship—and break up—with a woman none of them liked.

Despite all of the separation and distance, Ellie loved Sutton as much as she loved her brothers. She knew they would be able to pick their relationship up anytime, anywhere.

"Hey, Sutt," she said softly. Just saying his name made Ellie long for home, for their childhood, for the days filled with Cully that had ended too suddenly and too terribly. Sarah noticed her reaction and held her closer under the blanket.

"Elle," he replied. "I'm coming to get you. Let's go home."

* * *

"Sutton, what in the world is this thing?"

"It's a 1970 VW Westfalia Pop-top Camper Van," Sutton said. He crossed his arms over his chest in pride. He had known that Ellie would react this way at seeing the eclectic vehicle. It wasn't exactly practical, which was something that she valued. She always had. It's rugged, carefree, timelessness was the embodiment of Cully, though. If Sutton knew anything about his old friend, it was that she would need a little of that right about now. She would need it just as much as he would.

Sutton watched Ellie examine the camper with a skeptical eye. She put her fist up over her mouth and sighed as she looked at it. He almost laughed at the gesture. It was the same one she had been doing all of her life. He was only three years older than her, but was old enough to remember things that she didn't. Like when her family moved in next door. Seeing them was enough to send Sutton and his sisters into a tizzy. A family with three new playmates right next door. It was a kid's paradise. They had watched the Baxter's tumble out of their car one after the other. The two older boys pushing and shoving and running. Ellie was the youngest and the last out of the car. She was too tiny not to notice. Sutton had watched her walk towards the front door with pigtails and a scowl.

He was six, and she was three then. Ellie had eyed the house in the same way she eyed the camper now. Knuckles over her mouth like she was trying to force-feed herself the words to say in response to whatever it was she was looking at. Twenty-five years had come and gone taking the pigtails, leaving the scowl.

"Does it drive?" Ellie asked as she scratched at some rust on the handle of the front passenger door.

"Of course, it does! It got me here, didn't it?" Sutton said, putting his hand on his hip.

"Well, 'here' was only a five-hour drive. That's nothing. I know you think it's a long way since you never seem to want to make the trip, but it's not," Ellie said with a smile. Her words meant in jest stung all the same. "Now the drive that's ahead of us, well that's another story. Will this get us from Seattle to Denver, Sutton?" Ellie continued.

"It'll get us there," Sutton said as he brushed a speck of dirt off of the avocado green paint and then pulled her into a side-hug.

Ellie laughed at his effort towards cleanliness. It didn't matter what he did, the van had a perpetual appearance of dirt and disuse, and they both knew it. She eyed him and said, "Well, let's have the tour then."

"Here, she is!" Sutton said, smiling. "Home sweet home. For the next few days anyway. I've been calling her 'Maude' but, I'm open to changing her name. Thoughts?"

Ellie stepped inside and looked at the wood-paneled walls. There was a small bench seat with some kind of plastic fabric over it. The table in front of it was sturdy and scuffed, and the curtains hanging over the windows were gathered in the middle and held in place by dusty, frayed ties. The whole interior was a bland pallet of beige and brown.

The outside of the van was gaudy and ugly. The inside was boring and ugly.

"I think Maude fits her perfectly," Ellie said as she scrunched up her nose.

"Alright, a classic name for a classic vehicle," Sutton said as he sat on the bench seat like it was a throne.

"It's a little too classic if you ask me. Maybe we should just fly home, Sutton," Ellie sighed and squinted her brown eyes, trying to soften the blow of suggesting something different.

Sutton's heart sank at the thought of abandoning the road trip, at the thought of abandoning his last-ditch effort to honor Cully.

He leaned forward and sighed, elbows on his knees, eyes full of everything they both felt. Everything they knew they were going home to. "Elle, do you remember how Cully and I used to talk about spending the summer in one of these?" he asked quietly.

She nodded, fingering one of the frayed curtains. Her hands freed the dust that had clung to the fabric for years and it danced in the sunbeams streaming through the open door. Sutton watched it swirl and held back a sneeze.

"We never got to, Ellie," he said with a heartbreaking, straight-forward tone. "I hate that we never got to. I hate that we never got to do a lot of things. So, when I saw this camper van, I had to buy it, had to take it home. For Cully. Does that make sense, Ellie?"

"Oh, Sutton," she said, turning to him with a sad smile. "I understand completely. I hate this ugly thing, but I understand completely. Let's drive it home for Cully."

The knot in Sutton's stomach slowly dissolved, melted by Ellie's understanding. She held his gaze, the dust and light mingling between them, and he nodded his gratitude. She nodded in return and with the shake of her head, the plan was firmly in place.

"Open the glove box for me, Elle. There's a map in there. Take a look," Sutton said.

She did as he said and pulled out a map that looked to be an original fixture of the van. It smelled like library books and felt good and well used.

"Take a look at our route," he told her with excitement.

Ellie traced her finger along the route Sutton had highlighted.

"It'll take us a good three days or so to get home, but it'll be fun. I've planned out a few places to stop. Thought we might see a few people on the way."

Ellie looked at him skeptically. "Who are you thinking we'll see?"

"Well, we'll pick up Jake in Spokane and then head from there to Bozeman tonight. We'll spend the night in Bozeman with one of my old college buddies. He's got a huge house and offered us his guest rooms. We'll leave there tomorrow and drive down into Rocky Mountain National Park, spend the night at a cabin there, and then on to Denver the next morning."

"As long as I don't have to sleep in this thing," Ellie said as she eyed the frayed bench seat that converted into a bed behind her. She visibly cringed at the looks of it, and Sutton knew she would never spend a night on the filthy, old fabric.

"Don't worry, I won't make you suffer through a night with Maude, Ellie," Sutton replied, rolling his eyes.

Ellie sighed and sat down next to him. "Sutton, I want to go home. I need to go home."

He put his arm around her and pulled her to him. "Then let's go."

* * *

An hour later, they were on the road. Sarah had detained them longer than they had expected. "The cookies are almost ready," she had told them when they went inside to bring Ellie's bags to the car.

"You didn't need to make us cookies, Sarah," Ellie had told her with a smile and a hug.

"Speak for yourself," Sutton said as he began licking the beaters that were lying abandoned in the mixing bowl. "I'm Sutton, by the way."

Sarah had extended her hand and blushed as she shook his.

Sutton pretended not to notice like he always did when women reacted that way upon seeing him, and Ellie was grateful. Women didn't even need to know that he was a successful corporate lawyer with a bank account as big as his heart. His dark hair, square jaw, and striking green eyes were enough to make any woman gawk. Sarah was no different but she was easily embarrassed. Ellie was thankful for Sutton's graceful evasion. She didn't want to leave Sarah alone in the house with anything to overthink.

"Of course you need cookies. You can't go on a road trip without cookies and you can't grieve without comfort food," Sarah said, pulling her eyes away from Sutton. "Sutton, I'm so sorry for your loss. Ellie has told me all about how you all grew up together. I know he was one of your best friends and, I just can't imagine how you must be feeling right now…" She started to tear up again. Ellie pulled her into a hug and caught Sutton's gaze over Sarah's shoulder.

"Go get my bags," Ellie mouthed silently as she tilted her head towards the bedrooms down the hall.

Sutton, caught off guard by the amount of emotion in the kitchen, was happy to do as Ellie instructed.

Now, after a long and tearful goodbye on Sarah's end, they were finally off.

"Thanks again for the cookies, Sarah!" Sutton yelled out of the window as they pulled out of the driveway.

"Thanks for taking care of Ellie," Sarah yelled back.

Sutton looked at Ellie, winked, and then gave a Boy Scout salute to Sarah in a final goodbye.

"Sorry about all that," Ellie said softly.

"About all what?" Sutton asked

"All that emotion. Sarah is the kindest person I've ever met and sometimes she gets a little carried away with her nurturing nature."

"I thought it was nice," Sutton said. "Plus, we got some cookies out of it. Hand me one, would you?"

Ellie did as he asked and grabbed one for herself in the process. They were still warm and the chocolate left its mark on her fingers.

"So, Elle, how are you? Truly."

"I'm fine. How are you?"

"Come on, Ellie. Tell me."

"There's nothing to tell, Sutton. I just…am. I don't have anything to say."

"Then why did Sarah thank me for taking care of you? Do you need taking care of?" Sutton asked. She looked at him across the car. His hand was draped casually over the steering wheel, but his brow creased with concern and anxiety. That was Sutton. To the untrained eye, he looked like he was unflappable, but Ellie knew better. She knew him too well.

Ellie sighed, intent on reassuring him. "Sarah thinks everyone needs taking care of. She's a mother without a baby, Sutton. It's wonderful and endearing until she says something like that and makes you think that I need coddling."

Sutton laughed dryly. "Ellie, I've never known you to need coddling. We've also never been through anything like this, though. It's ok if you need taking care of."

"I don't need it any more than you do," She said, teasing him.

Sutton let out another dry laugh as Ellie took a bite of her cookie. It was delicious and chocolaty and tasted like childhood. Like their childhood. The one they had all shared. Now it was all crushed and shattered and colored in sepia tones.

All of their memories were touched with sadness now. Forever. There would always be something missing for all of them.

Ellie looked at Sutton. Truly looked at him for the first time since he had stepped out of this awful thing in her driveway. He looked unkempt. Bedraggled. Worn down. He had a day's worth of growth on his chin, and his green eyes looked just as raw and scratchy. She could tell he had been crying but didn't want to point it out and embarrass him.

Mostly, he looked tired. And sad. So sad. As sad as she felt. She knew he would. Cully's death meant just as much to him as it did to her.

Ellie grew silent, digesting Sutton's road trip plans. She had known since this morning that her brother Jake would be joining them. That was one of the few details she could recall from her mother's call. Well, that detail and the one about Cully.

Jake and Sutton were the same age. Exactly the same age, actually. Not long after the Baxters moved in next door to the Pierces this fun fact was discovered. It wasn't all that revolutionary. People share birthdays all the time, but the kids all saw it as further evidence that the friendships were meant to be. For years, July 20th saw the biggest joint birthday party the neighborhood had ever seen. The gate between their yards was left open, each mother sharing hostess duties, each birthday boy rallying the hordes of kids into party games and mischief.

Jake and Sutton had shared a grade, shared a birthday, even shared a few sports championships in high school but without Cully, they were like the two back wheels on a tricycle—balanced, content, but motionless.

"I haven't talked to Jake at all. Have you?" Ellie asked, breaking the easy silence.

"We haven't talked since yesterday. I called him right after I hung up with Rose."

Rose. Ellie hadn't even talked to her yet. She hadn't talked to anyone but her mom. After The Call, she had just shut herself in her room and couldn't remember what happened after that.

"How is Rose?"

"I can't talk about Rose right now, Ellie," Sutton said evenly. "I can't think about all of that."

Ellie understood. Of course, she understood.

"Grief is so odd, isn't it? Everyone wants you to talk about it. But words can't contain it, you know?"

Sutton looked at Ellie and shook his head slowly. He offered her a half-smile and said, "You always know just how to say it don't you, Elle?"

"I didn't say anything. That's the point of what I'm saying. The fact that I'm not, that *we're* not saying anything is the point of what I'm saying," Ellie said laughing.

"Exactly," Sutton said.

Exactly.

That was enough for now. It was enough that someone else understood and that someone else didn't want to talk about it.

"Do you want to sit here quietly then?" Ellie asked softly.

"Not really. I don't want to talk about everything, but I would like to talk about something," Sutton said with a shrug. His right hand was draped easily over the weathered steering wheel while the other grabbed for another cookie. "How about this. I'll ask you how you are, and you answer like none of this ever happened. Answer the way you would have if I asked you yesterday. Before…Cully." Sutton eyed Ellie and cleared his throat before looking back at the road.

"Ok, I will if you will," Ellie told him with a sly smile.

"I will," Sutton said, shrugging yet again. Like Ellie's words and suspicions could be brushed off and rolled aside as easily as good posture.

"Well, yesterday I would have told you that I'm doing well. Work is good. We've begun rehearsals for the Holiday season. The pieces are challenging but not terribly so. It should be beautiful once we're ready," Ellie said with a satisfied smile.

"Everything you play is always beautiful, Elle. That's why you play for the Seattle Symphony Orchestra." Sutton smiled at Ellie with all sincerity.

"I saw your guitar in the back. I brought my violin if you want to play something together later. Like when we were kids," Ellie said with a note of hope in her voice.

"I don't think I could keep up with you, Ellie. Not anymore."

"Nonsense," she began but her protest was cut off by the sound of her phone ringing. Trace Jones's name lit up the screen, sending a jolt through Ellie's whole body.

"Who is it?" Sutton asked without looking over at her.

Ellie cleared her throat and stared nervously at the screen. "It's no one," She said, a note of indecision in her voice.

"No one, huh?" Sutton said suspiciously. He turned his head towards her, a sly smile on his lips. "No one must be the name of whoever sent you those roses I saw on your bedside table earlier."

Ellie turned, eyes flashing and cheeks blushing towards Sutton. "Maybe," she said simply. She had no intention of diving into everything with Sutton. It was risky enough to dive into a new relationship. No need to make it worse by broadcasting it. The phone continued to ring.

"Answer it, Elle. I promise I won't eavesdrop too badly," Sutton turned his head and feigned disinterest, but she saw the smile that still lingered in his eyes. He and her brothers had always relished teasing her about how nervous she got about new relationships. Some things never changed.

She took a deep breath and answered the call. "Hello," Ellie said softly.

"Hi, Ellie," Trace's voice poured gently into her ears like hot water in a coffee pot—deep and rich and warm, causing emotion to brew within her. "How are you this morning?"

"I'm doing fine, thank you for asking. And thank you for the roses. They were beautiful."

"It was the least I could do. I hoped you would see the flowers and know that I'm here for you. The last thing anyone needs is to be alone while they're grieving."

Ellie couldn't help but smile at his words, letting the implication of what he was saying sink in. Perhaps he wasn't just trying to be kind. Perhaps he was pressing in, pushing his suit, pursuing her with kindness and comfort. "You're so thoughtful, Trace. Thank you."

"So are you holding up ok? Can I come and take you to coffee, get your mind off of things? I'm not leaving Seattle until tomorrow morning and I'd love nothing more than to spend some time with you before I leave."

Ellie's heart sank. She would have loved that too. "I wish I could, but I'm on my way home. For the funeral. Sutton came and picked me up this morning."

"Oh, of course, of course. Umm…" Trace hesitated and cleared his throat. When he spoke again, Ellie heard the slightest hint of insecurity. Doubt. "Is Sutton another brother of yours?"

Ellie smiled, trying not to laugh. He was jealous! Trace Jones was jealous of Sutton! "No, he's not my brother. He's as good as one, though. His family lived next door to mine all growing up. They still do, actually, and his sister Rose is…was… married to Cully. The one that…" She couldn't say it, couldn't continue, and thankfully Trace cut in and saved her.

"I see!" The relief was obvious in his tone. "So you're driving home together then. I'm glad. As I said, I don't want you to be alone."

"Thank you, Trace. I appreciate your calling. I'm sorry things worked out this way. I was looking forward to getting to know you better," Ellie blushed as she said it, very aware that Sutton was listening.

"I'm the one who's sorry, Ellie. I'll call you soon after you've had a chance to process things a little more."

"I'd like that," Ellie said softly with a smile.

"And Ellie," Trace added. "I'll be thinking about you until then."

She smiled and hung up, allowing herself to feel the glow of his words.

"Well," Sutton cut in. "He seems nice."

"He does, doesn't he?" Ellie said wistfully and she meant it. He did seem nice. "They all do at first, though."

Sutton laughed. "I don't know, that was the biggest bouquet I've ever seen. A man doesn't spend that much on flowers if he isn't invested."

"Oh, he has plenty of money to spend. I wouldn't read too much into that," Ellie said waving Sutton off.

"What does he do to make all this money, Elle?"

"He's a musician," Ellie said dismissively. She didn't want to talk about Trace. Didn't want to invest energy into something like that right now. Not when her heart was so shattered and not when Sutton's had been too. "Enough about me. How are you? I haven't seen you in a while. You didn't come home last Christmas. Or the one before."

"I had other commitments, Ellie." Sutton's jaw twitched a little when he said it. The change in his demeanor was staggering. Ellie knew why. Regret did that to a person. It caused nerves and anxiety and twitches.

"Sutton, you don't need to feel bad about working hard. Or about trying to make a relationship work. You're thirty-one years old. That's what you're supposed to be doing," Ellie said. She reached across the car and rubbed his shoulder. The way Rose would have done if she was there.

Sutton didn't take his eyes off of the road. Just kept staring out at the bumper of the car ahead of them on the interstate. "I don't feel bad about it. I do feel mad about it, though. I've spent the last four years working hard and trying to make a relationship work. Missed Christmas and every other holiday with everyone while doing it, and I have nothing to show for it."

"What do you mean you have nothing to show for it? You're a lawyer, Sutton. A lawyer at one of the top firms in Portland. I know that Kate breaking things off this spring was awful and came as a shock to you, but otherwise, you're doing great! We're all so proud of you." Ellie smiled and squeezed his shoulder one more time for good measure.

"Why do you say her name like that?" Sutton asked defensively.

"What?" Ellie asked blindsided by his tone. "Who's name like what?"

"Kate's name. You said it in a tone. A bad tone."

"I did not."

"You did. You all never liked her," Sutton said under his breath.

"Not a single one of us ever told you we didn't like her," Ellie said through blushing cheeks. It didn't matter. Sutton, being the discerning lawyer that he was, didn't need her blush to give her away. Her carefully worded response was telling enough.

"You never told me, but you sure told each other," He said with a scoff.

"Fine. We might have all agreed that she was the worst, but we never would have told you that!" Ellie said with wide eyes.

"The worst? Honestly Ellie. I dated her for four years. We nearly got married!" Sutton said with an eye roll.

"And thank God you didn't! I couldn't stand the way that she always gave your mom those annoying half-smiles. Your mother is the funniest woman I've ever met! There's something wrong with a person that can't give your mother a full smile. I would understand if Kate had ugly teeth that she was trying to keep hidden. She didn't though! Her teeth were perfectly lovely. Her whole face was perfectly lovely. I can give her that, and it explains how you could have missed so many of her flaws, but truly, Sutton. Did you really want to marry a woman who couldn't even find enough joy in life to smile with her teeth showing?"

Ellie stopped flailing her arms long enough to cross them over her chest. She looked at Sutton, awaiting his response. He didn't say anything, just stewed in silence while his jaw muscles chewed on Ellie's words.

"She wasn't right for you, Sutton. She just wasn't," Ellie said softly.

"Well, at least the two of you can agree on that," he said simply.

"Forget about her and all of the Christmas's she stole from us. How is everything else? Your mom told me you bought a house! Tell me about it!" Ellie said with brightness in her tone.

"It's fine, Ellie. Want to listen to some music?" Sutton asked sadly.

"Umm, sure. Music is fine," She replied skeptically.

Sutton turned the dial on the radio and didn't say another word.

Chapter 3

ELLIE HAD BEEN ASLEEP FOR AN HOUR. IT WAS FOR the best. It kept her from asking too many questions. Questions that he didn't want to answer yet.

As he glanced at her across the van, he realized that he had a few questions for her, though. He hadn't seen her in months. Not since she had moved to Seattle and landed her dream job.

Even a year and a half later, he was still shocked that Ellie had left home. She wasn't a wanderer by nature. She was more of a "grow where you're planted" kind of person, and she had been firmly planted in the suburban Colorado neighborhood of their childhood.

She had done it, though—sought out a change, left everyone behind, and built a life for herself. He was surprised by the contentment and peace he sensed in her. He wanted to know how she had found it. For now, though, he would let her rest.

Rest was good for a broken heart, and Sutton knew just how shattered hers was. She hadn't said so, hadn't even appeared so, but he knew.

Cully had been her hero, and now they all had to live without him.

Sutton pulled out his phone and snapped a picture of Ellie, head lolling, chin touching her chest. She had never been a graceful sleeper, something that had been a running joke between their two families for years.

The road was straighter than an arrow for the next little stretch, and he felt confident enough about sending a text while he was driving. Ellie would have scolded if she was awake, though.

He put the picture of his slumbering co-pilot into the group text between the Baxter's and Pierce's with the caption: "Sleeping Beauty at it again." He hit send and sighed, hoping that the picture would bring a smile to everyone. They all needed it.

Sutton's Dad Samuel was the first to reply. "Eyes on the road, Sutton! We need you two safe and sound!"

From Ellie's Dad, Peter: "Don't be too hard on him, Samuel. Who could resist staring at such a beautiful girl!"

From Rose: "Love you two"

From Sutton's Mom, Janine: "A Gentleman would have strapped her forehead to the seat…"

From Ellie's mom, Lisa: "Is that chocolate on her face? That girl!"

From Sutton: "Too many chocolate chip cookies. She's out like a light."

From Jake: "When are you getting to my house? I don't know if my laundry will be done in time."

From Sutton's sister Pippa: "Jake, you know how to do laundry?"

Sutton smiled at the stream, trying not to notice Cully's absence.

"I'll be careful, Dad. Jake, we'll be there in three hours. Don't forget the fabric softener!" Sutton replied.

He put his phone in his pocket, ready to focus on the road again. They had driven only an hour, but they felt as far away from the city as possible. The evergreen state stretched out around them, the dark hues of pine standing out under the gray skies above.

They would reach Snoqualmie Falls any minute now, and he didn't want to miss it. He had seen the falls once before when he and Kate had gone to visit Jake a few years back. She was underwhelmed by their majesty. Probably because of the argument they were in. She was always one to sulk after a fight.

Being raised in Colorado had trained Sutton never to miss natural beauty, though. There was something deep within him that pulled him to it, made him notice. Of truth be told, he depended on nature's wonders and beauty. He knew that Ellie was the same. She had lived near the ocean for the last year and a half, but she was a Colorado girl at heart. She would love the falls with their cliffs and mountains and staggering beauty.

Ten minutes later, Sutton put Maude in park in the visitor lot and shook Ellie awake.

"Get up, Elle. Let's stretch our legs."

She awoke with a start and stretched her arms wide above her head. Sutton watched her yawn and noticed that she did have chocolate on her face. He held back a laugh and waited for her to wake up enough to get out of the car.

"Where are we?" She asked sleepily.

"Snoqualmie Falls. I thought we could take a few minutes to stretch our legs and see it."

"Sounds great!" She said. "Oh wait, I have a million text messages to catch up on," Ellie said as she climbed out of the van. She unlocked her phone to find the humiliating picture Sutton had sent to everyone.

"Sutton Pierce! You're heartless!" She said, shoving him a little.

He laughed and said, "Your mom is very observant. You do have chocolate on your face."

Her hands immediately went to her face as she ducked to peak in the rearview mirror hanging by a thread off of the passenger door. She turned her face from side to side until she found the offending mark and wiped it off with her finger. "There," she said with more sass than her eyes held.

Sutton laughed. "Much better. Do you want to pose for another picture to avenge your honor? I'll even send it to your mystery man."

She rolled her eyes at him and gave him a little shove. "Let's just go."

The September air was wet and cold, filled with the water that made everything around them lush and green. It had taken Sutton a long time to get used to the heavy air of the Pacific Northwest. In Colorado, each breath was crisp, unencumbered by moisture. It was weightless. Imperceptible. Those who weren't used to it called it thin but, he knew better. It was pure and simple. Just the way Sutton liked things.

Here though, just like in Portland, the air carried things. Water and fog and pine and mist. It was never alone. Always dragging things along with it. He supposed it was good. It made for some beautiful scenery. His skin was never dry. But there was a denseness to it. He had always felt like he was pulling too much into his lungs. Like even breathing was too complex here.

He sighed as they walked towards the observation deck, ducking below the canopies of trees, swerving around people in their hiking boots and sweaters. The dirt crunched beneath his shoes, and he enjoyed the sound, enjoyed it even more with Ellie there.

"What are you thinking about, Sutt?" She asked as she shoved her hands in her coat pocket. It was a deep green color. Evergreen. Like her. Unchanged. He had noticed it when she got in the car back in Seattle. She seemed not to have changed. Her appearance hadn't anyway. Her hair was still the same chestnut brown, long, straight, silky. Her eyes the same icey blue. Her hands were still works of art, long tapered fingers that pulled music out of strings and ivory and brass. She had always been a work of art, something to admire.

Ellie had matured, though. She held herself with contentment and composure. That was new. The last time he had seen her, she had seemed frazzled and fearful of the future. It wasn't a mark of weakness or anything, just a mark of youth. She had grown up in the last few years, and he was curious as to how it had happened.

"I'm thinking about the air," Sutton said as he turned his attention from her. "I don't like the air here."

She laughed and said, "This is some of the purest air you'll find. What do you mean you don't like it?"

"It's too wet. It feels…excessive," He said with a shrug.

"Hmm. I suppose. It smells good, though. Doesn't it? Like pine trees and rain. It smells almost melancholy," Ellie replied as she closed her eyes, took a deep breath, and exhaled.

"How can something smell melancholy?" Sutton asked. He kicked a rock out of the dirt path. It landed under a tree, and he wondered how long it would stay in that exact place. Probably for years. Moss would grow on it. Insects would burrow below it. It would be the foundation of a whole ecosystem and all because it was kicked there with no intention by a random person.

Nature always mined intention out of the unintentional. Perhaps that was why it was so comforting.

Ellie's voice pulled him away from his mind's meandering. "You know what I mean. This smell just makes you want to curl up with tea and a book and a blanket. Maybe open the windows and listen to the rain while you have a good cry. At least that's what I want to do," She paused for a minute and sniffed sharply. "I won't though. Instead, I'll walk with my old friend and look at some amazing waterfalls. Then I'll get back into the ugliest car known to man and drive home."

Sutton was caught off guard by her taciturn speech. He was struggling to read her.

"Ellie, do you want to cry? I mean do you want to do all of those things? We can if you want," he said. They followed a bend in the path, leading them closer to the falls. Sutton could hear them off in the distance.

"No. I don't really know what I want to do, Sutton. My brother died. I don't know what you're supposed to do after that," She laughed dryly and shrugged with her hands still in her pockets. "I probably should do all that melodramatic stuff. It seems like the thing to do. I just don't want to, though you know? You don't want to talk and I don't want to sulk so this seems like as good a thing to do as any."

Sutton nodded.

They fell into silent steps beside each other, letting the sound of the waterfalls grow louder in their ears. The sound was crushing. Powerful. Constant. It was just the thing he craved.

There were far fewer people on the path than he expected. It made sense. The day was dismal at best. Cold and wet.

The last time he had been here, the sound of the crowds had overpowered the rushing water at this point in the walk. There had been tourist after tourist in front of him and Kate. One in particular had been smoking a cigarette. The smoke kept blowing back in his face, and it had driven him crazy. Kate had seen that he was annoyed by the way he had worked the muscles in his jaw. She had rolled her eyes at him and chided him for being so "crotchety."

That's always how it had been with them. They had never cared about the same things.

He inhaled deeply. Whatever his complaints were about the air today, at least he didn't smell cigarette smoke.

The path opened up ahead of them leading to the lower observation deck just as heavy rain began to fall. Trees perched around the railing. Maples and spruces held tight by their roots as they leaned out towards the water. He smiled to himself as the sight appeared. He didn't mind the rain. It felt refreshing and fitting and he understood Ellie's comment about melancholy smells.

"Last one there buys lunch," Ellie said as she suddenly took off running towards the deck. There was not another soul in sight, and Sutton took her bait.

"You're on!"

They took off at a sprint, determined to beat each other. The deck was about one hundred yards ahead of them, and their strides closed the distance at rapid speed. The rain fell hard on their faces, pouring down their cheeks like tears.

Sutton breathed deep, lungs and muscles burning. His mind flashed back to their childhood, running through spring rain on the way home from school. All six of them disrupting puddles and splashing each other along. The memories came fast and unwelcome, memories of Rose and Cully ahead of him, holding hands and laughing as they led everyone home through the deluge. Of Cully turning and waving them all along, then kicking water up at him as he passed by. His mind saw the picture, but his heart felt the closeness, the connection, the childlike joy of knowing how to dance to the rhythm of storms.

Sutton forced the thoughts away, buried his rage and pain at the bottom of his chest, let it lie there and smolder out with every step he took. The running felt good. It made the rest of his body burn and ache until he stopped noticing the pain he had been feeling since yesterday. Until his heart wasn't the only muscle that felt like it was on fire.

He was only a few strides away from the deck, and he stole a glance over his shoulder at Ellie. She had a scowl on her face and was running with all her might. He almost laughed at how seriously she was taking their foot race, but he stopped himself. Maybe she was running away from the heart ache too.

"You aren't going to win, Elle," Sutton yelled through the rain. He stepped foot on the deck ready to claim first place, but as he did, his feet slipped out from under him. The rain-soaked deck was as slippery as ice, and he skated right off. He landed hard in the mud just in time for Ellie to stop in front of him, just short of the deck.

"Pride comes before a fall, Sutton," She said with a smile on her face.

Sutton looked down at his hands, his pants, his jacket. They were all covered in mud. Thick, wet, mud. It oozed through his fingers and felt good in all of its messiness. He turned his head up at Ellie and feigned a deep, dramatic scowl. "Now, Ellie, I'm hurt that you would start mudslinging while I'm laid out here like this. You should leave that to me," Sutton said as he scooped up a handful of mud and threw it at her. It landed right on her chest and splattered like a paintball.

She looked down at her ruined coat, eyes and mouth wide, but Sutton knew what was coming. He had gotten a rise out of Ellie Baxter enough times to know that she could dish it as well as she could take it.

Without saying a word, She bent down and grabbed two handfuls of mud. They found their mark on Sutton's face. "Your aim has improved, Ellie," he told her as he scrambled to his feet and threw another mudball.

"I'm like fine wine, Sutton. I get better every year!" She threw another round of mud, and it landed on his pants.

"I think I proved that I can still best you at a foot race, though," Sutton yelled through another onslaught of rain and mud. "Admit that you lost and I'll stop!"

"I'll admit that I lost but you have to buy me lunch anyway. For your lack of manners out here," Ellie said. They were both laughing hysterically by now. Laughing and wiping mud out of their eyes.

"Fine!" Sutton said breathlessly, hands in the air in surrender. "Truce?"

"Truce," Ellie giggled back. "Should we finally pay attention to these glorious waterfalls? I think we owe it to our outfits to at least make the suffering they've endured worth something."

Sutton took a deep breath, relishing the feeling of laughter, and nodded. They walked carefully over to the edge of the railing, awestruck by the view of Snoqualmie Falls in front of them.

The crest of the twin falls appeared, each veering around a giant rock in the center, curving their way around to meet on the other side. Once they joined in the middle, they fell in graceful pillars in the distance. Their waters tumbling down in an unstoppable display and crashed together at the bottom.

They looked reckless and beautiful.

"I feel like we're those falls, Sutton," Ellie said, still gasping for breath as she leaned on the railing. The rain punctuated her words like a staccato mark over each one. "Without Cully, I feel like we're falling over rocks and cliffs, crashing down, and no one can stop us."

Sutton didn't take his eyes off of the falls. Didn't stop looking at the foam and mist and white, gushing water at the bottom. He just nodded and sighed. Nodded and sighed and pulled her to him in a hug. "Yeah, well at least there's two of them, huh Elle? At least they're not crashing down alone."

She nodded.

They stayed there like that, then. Allowing the rain to wash off all the mud and letting the water crash in contained recklessness ahead. They stayed there together, and then they walked back to the van in easy silence.

Chapter 4

"STILL HAVEN'T BOUGHT YOURSELF A PROPER suitcase huh, Jake?" Ellie said eyeing the trash bag that her brother Jake had slung over his shoulder.

They had made it to his apartment, still slightly damp from their trip to Snoqualmie Falls. In typical Jake fashion, he didn't even question them about it, leaving them to ask if they could use his apartment to change. Now, finally, dry with her hair pulled back in a ponytail, Ellie stood in the hallway of his apartment complex, a dingy and poorly lit corridor that smelled of too much cheap cologne.

Her brother was much the same as the last time she had seen him a few months before. Handsome and sloppy. Carefree and big-hearted. He had been living in this apartment complex for about a year now. It was rundown and unremarkable, but it fit Jake. Even though he had developed a few different apps and sold them for a very good amount of money, he still lived like a poor college kid. He said he had no desire to spend his money. Didn't even have any desire to have it, really. What he was really after was the freedom that being wealthy afforded him. He spent his days playing the piano, skiing, and rock climbing.

"Why would I buy a suitcase when I have a regular supply of trash bags?" Jake said in all seriousness as they walked towards the door. " I've been trying to tell you guys for years that the trash bag is the most useful and versatile invention known to mankind, I mean humankind. Sorry, sis. Didn't mean to offend you or women in general there." Jake said eyeing Ellie apologetically.

His last girlfriend had done a number on him.

"I'm not offended by the term 'mankind' Jake," Ellie said with an eye-roll. "I am offended by that trash bag, though. Apologize for that."

"Listen," Jake continued as they made their way down the stairs towards the battered front door of Jake's building. "Trash bags are cheap. You can get a whole box for ten bucks and then use them for everything! Suitcase, clothes hamper, storage, table cloth, poncho, mattress protector, and yes, even trash."

Ellie stifled a giggle as Sutton nodded his head, raised his eyebrows, and said, "I wonder why society at large hasn't caught on to these benefits, Jake?"

"Because society at large is full of elitist, capitalistic consumers that's why," Jake replied with a shrug.

"Or maybe it's because society at large isn't as cheap as you," Sutton said with a playful shove.

"I don't know, Sutt it looks to me like Jake's trash bag and Maude are a match made in heaven," Ellie said as she tugged open the door of the van. She had to shout for her words to be heard over the screech the hinges made. "I think I'm the only one that's too classy for this trip."

"You didn't look too classy in that picture Sutton sent of you earlier, Elle," Jake said with a wink at Sutton and the two of them laughed in response.

"Fine, we're all a match made in heaven. Can we go now?" Ellie said laughing as she climbed in behind the wheel. Sutton settled into the passenger seat and Jake lounged on the bench seat in the back.

She started the van, something that amazed them all even if they didn't say so—and steered it east.

"So, Sutton where'd you get this beaut?" Jake asked as he rubbed his hand over the cheap, faded upholstery.

"He bought it for this trip," Ellie replied, looking at Jake behind her in the cracked mirror hanging from the center of the windshield. "We're supposed to be having an adventure."

"Got any plans for it once we get home?" Jake said as he looked around with appreciation.

"Not yet," Sutton said, eying Ellie with a knowing smile. "Why?"

They both knew what Jake was about.

"I might be interested in taking it off of your hands. If you'd be willing to let me make payments, that is."

Ellie laughed and rolled her eyes at Jake. "What for, Jake?"

"I have a few plans. A portable house might come in handy," Jake said with a shrug.

"What is it this time?" Sutton asked. His tone was full of genuine curiosity. He knew that whatever Jake was going to say, it would be interesting in the least.

"I want to follow the butterfly migration in the spring. Watch them fly, you know?"

Jake looked out the window of the van, wistfully. Hopelessly. Ellie watched him through the rearview mirror, sensing what was on his mind.

She knew her big brother well. He seemed like a lost soul, ever wandering, but he wasn't aimless. He was just different than most. Where her life had always followed one long, straight trajectory from where she was and where she was going, Jake's was more like the path of a boomerang. Short stints, jaunts towards one thing or another, and then he would make his way back home again.

It frustrated their father to no end, and it worried their mother even more, but Ellie just knew. Knew that was who Jake was.

Ellie turned her eyes on the road but her mind was on her brother behind her. Her heart broke ever so slightly. He was making his way back home again, but would he be able to launch back out? Would he be able to wander and adventure and marvel at the world as he did before? After the anchor of it all had come lose would he feel as untethered as she did?

Or would he find things too hollow now? Too broken to send him out again?

He wanted to watch the butterflies, wanted to watch something that had transformed find its way. He wanted to see something fly after life had changed it.

Ellie understood.

* * *

The six-hour trek from Spokane to Bozeman was uneventful. Ellie drove the first two hours, Jake the second, and Sutton the last.

They pulled into town just as the sun was setting, and the colorful sky stopped them all in their tracks.

"Pull over!" Ellie said, breaking the easy silence that had descended over the car. "We need to watch the sunset! Like, really watch it, not just look every few seconds while we drive."

Jake and Sutton didn't protest. Some little piece of Sutton's soul felt known the moment that Ellie said that. He looked at her with a smile and nod and pulled the van onto the side of the road.

Few cars drove by, zooming by in a soft whir as the three pulled their tired bodies out onto the patch of dead grass. The sky was streaked in light and color, and the air held the crisp hint of autumn. Sutton breathed in slowly, deeply, as they stood and watched.

Ellie was in the middle, Sutton and Jake on either side. She grabbed each of their hands and squeezed them tight. It was one of her age-old gestures, what she always did when she didn't want to talk but wanted someone to know that she loved them. Sutton squeezed her hand back in return, struck by her soft, delicate fingers.

"Elle, remember when we were little, and you used to call the sunset 'sky sleeps'?" Sutton asked.

Ellie blushed and smiled at him. "It makes sense, doesn't it? The sky goes to sleep when the sun sets."

"I used to laugh every time you said it," Jake added, looking at Ellie. He had turned his battered baseball cap backward so he could better see the pinks and yellows and purples in front of him. "Cully gave me what for for that."

"He did?" Ellie said. Sutton heard such sadness in her voice.

"He told me I shouldn't laugh at you. Said it would make you stop saying what you think."

Tears filled Ellie's eyes at Jake's words, and she sniffed loudly, trying to keep them at bay.

Something visceral squeezed tight within Sutton's gut at the sight of her tears. He hated it when women cried, but he especially hated it when Ellie did. Perhaps it was because she never cried over irrational things. She gave her emotions freely, but she never wasted them. Her tears only fell for worthy causes and this was certainly one of them.

"Oh, Elle, don't cry," Sutton said softly as he pulled her into a hug.

It was hardly the first time he had hugged her. A lifetime of friendship had afforded plenty of occasions, but over the last few years, he had allowed a distance to creep in between them. A distance that was meant to keep Kate happy. She had always been the jealous type, and when she had met Ellie for the first time, she had made her hatred of his beautiful and disarming childhood friend clear.

"There's no way you two can be just friends. She's far too attractive, Sutton," Kate had said on the plane ride back to Portland.

"I don't understand what you mean," Sutton had said in annoyance. "I don't see Ellie that way. She's like a sister."

"That might have worked when you were kids, but not any-more, Sutton. She's a beautiful woman, and there's no way you don't know it."

At the time, Sutton had been confused by Kate's assessment. Ellie was like a sister. Of course, Sutton knew she was beautiful, but he had never thought of her like that. Still, he had done what Kate had asked and had stopped showing any kind of affection for Ellie ever since.

Now, though, with Kate long gone and, moved by Ellie's tears, he held her close and was surprised that Kate's words dropped into his mind. *"She's a beautiful woman, and there's no way you don't know it."*

Suddenly, Sutton was very aware that a woman was in his arms, a woman and not just Ellie. Before he could stop himself, he noticed how her cheek felt resting against his chest, how narrow and soft the small of her back felt under his hand, how her hair smelled like berries and vanilla. Before his mind could catch up to his senses, though Ellie pulled away, completely unaware of the unexpected thoughts racing through Sutton's mind.

"What would I do without you two?" she said softly.

"Probably fly home like a normal person," Sutton replied as he cleared his throat, desperate to force some normalcy and humor into the moment.

They smiled and then watched the sun settle behind the hori-zon. Watched it go to sleep.

"We should be on our way, I'm starving!" Jake finally said, thrusting his hands into his pockets for warmth.

"Troy said that he would have dinner waiting for us," Sutton said as they piled into the car. He was more than ready to leave the sunset and the moment it had caused on the side of the road. Only too ready to forget how Ellie had felt in his arms.

"Sutt, is this the same Troy that was your college roommate?"

Ellie asked him while she buckled her seatbelt, apprehension blossoming on her face.

"Yeah, he came home with me for spring break one year. We all went skiing. Remember?" Sutton replied as he shifted Maude into gear and began driving.

"That's the friend who's house we're staying at?" Ellie asked in horror. Jake's reaction was quite the opposite, though. He laughed loudly, too loudly. Ellie tried to reach into the backseat to smack him, but her arms couldn't span the distance.

"Yeah, what's wrong with that?" Sutton asked in confusion. "You seemed to get along just fine that trip."

"Should I tell him then, Elle?" Jake said. By this time, tears of laughter were streaming down his face, and he was doubled over the old brown seat belt.

Ellie didn't reply and instead looked out the window so Sutton wouldn't see the deep blush on her cheeks.

"Troy was Ellie's first kiss. On the ski lift during that trip," Jake said.

Sutton looked towards Ellie, still confused. That was nothing to be embarrassed about. She must have been sixteen or seventeen at the time. True, that was a little old for a first kiss, but Ellie had always been picky and never really dated. Troy wasn't' who Sutton would have picked for her. He was far from good enough, just like every other man, but it was in the past. So what?

"That's nothing to be embarrassed about, Ellie," Sutton said finally with a shrug.

"No, the kiss wasn't. Falling getting off of the ski lift afterward was, though," Jake said through a fresh round of laughter.

"I didn't fall!" Ellie said defensively. "My coat snagged on the chairlift and it pulled me along behind it around the other side."

Sutton pictured the whole affair and tried not to laugh along with Jake. This was obviously a painful memory for her, and he was trying to be understanding.

"They had to stop the lift and get me untangled. I was mortified! The worst part of it all though was the fact that Troy saw the whole thing and then didn't talk to me the rest of the day!"

"He didn't try to help you up?" Sutton asked incredulously.

"No! He didn't ask for my number or anything afterward either! Just pretended like the kiss and the fall never even happened," Ellie said quietly with her arms crossed over her chest. "Jake only knows because he was on the seat behind us and saw the whole thing."

"It was quite the show, Elle," Jake said as he sighed in that contended way that comes after a fit of laughter. He reached up and squeezed her shoulder in reassurance. "Don't worry. He's probably forgotten the whole thing."

"Well, I sure haven't," Ellie said under her breath.

Sutton sat quietly digesting the whole story. Why hadn't Troy mentioned anything to him about Ellie throughout all of these years? Perhaps it was because he knew that Sutton had always viewed her like a little sister. Maybe he thought Sutton would have been protective?

Looking at Ellie across the car now, still stewing and angry over something that had happened over a decade ago, confirmed that Troy was right. Sutton did feel protective. Protective and responsible.

"Elle, I didn't know. I'm sorry. Should we skip this stop? Camp somewhere?" Sutton said. Concern laced his tone, and her features softened.

"It's fine, Sutton. I would have told you, but it's one of my more embarrassing anecdotes. Let's just go. I'm sure he's a perfectly nice person now, and I would hate for you to miss out on seeing a friend."

"I can catch him another time. Let's just skip it," Sutton offered again.

"No," Ellie said, adamant this time. "I can't let myself slip into insecurity. I'm a grown woman with a lot to show for myself. I'm not going to cower just because he made me feel terrible about myself when I was a teenager." Her confidence seemed forced, but it was there all the same.

Sutton looked at the fire in her eyes and didn't dare question her. She was right, after all. She was an impressive woman in every way. Beautiful. Talented. Composed, despite her current outburst. Why not give her a chance to show Troy what he missed out on?

"Alright. If you're sure," Sutton said gently.

"She's sure," Jake said loudly. "Just don't ever ask her to go skiing again."

Chapter 5

Standing on the doorstep of Troy's Bozeman mansion Ellie told herself to stay calm. She had meant every word she had said to Sutton. She had no reason to cower because of some distant teenage memory.

Her confidence began to wane, though as the door swung open to the autumn evening framing Troy in light and warmth.

"You made it!" he said as he and Sutton hugged in that masculine way men do—all pats and shoulders.

"Thanks for having us, man," Sutton said in his easy way. "The place looks spectacular!"

They made their way into the foyer of the grand home. Filled with masculine wood and dark furnishings, it bespoke rustic wealth. Ellie didn't know whether she should be impressed or put off.

Jake was obviously the latter. She could see the wheels in his head turning. Elitist. Showy. Obnoxious. That's what he would be thinking. He managed a polite nod in Troy's direction, though, and Ellie knew her mother would be proud.

When Troy's gaze landed upon her, she couldn't help but blush furiously.

Unfortunately, he was still just as good looking as he had been on that ski lift. Only now he was rich too.

Ellie knew it was a complete cliché, knew that as an independent, grown woman, she should laugh at her girlish desire to impress him for his looks and money, but her heart was in a state of shock and confusion over Cully. She couldn't rely on It to stand up with its usual fortitude.

Thankfully, Jake and Sutton were there, and the thought of giving Jake another chapter of this whole Troy saga to laugh at was enough to put some mettle in her spine.

"Thank you so much for the invitation to stay, Troy. It's nice to see you again," Ellie finally said. She hoped her tone came across as polite. It sounded more wooden in her ears, though.

"Again? Have we met? I'm sure I would have remembered," Troy said, his flashy, movie star smile faltering ever so slightly. He looked her up and down slowly, lingering overlong at times.

Jake immediately snorted in laughter and tried to hide it by clearing his throat. Ellie simply blinked, trying not to let her surprise show. She had obviously inherited the lion's share of the family's subtly.

"Only briefly. Years ago," she said with a polite smile. She was obviously forgettable, so very forgettable, but she would never let it be said of her that she wasn't gracious. Not when she was Lisa Baxter's daughter.

Sutton put his hand on the small of her back and let it rest there in a silent show of support. "Ellie went skiing with us that year over spring break, Troy. I'm sure you remember."

"Yeah sure, skiing. That sounds right," Troy said dismissively. "We'll have to reminisce over dinner."

He led them into the dining room, making a point to show them the photographs on the walls as they walked.

"These are a few of my earlier works," he said, pointing to a large black and white picture of an oak tree hanging in the hallway. He stopped to look at it, clearly in awe of himself. They nearly bumped into him as he abruptly stopped to gawk. "I like to keep them here to remind myself of how far I've come. How much I've grown."

"So down to earth," Jake said sarcastically. Troy didn't pick up on it, but Sutton tried to smooth things over nonetheless.

"Are you still photographing landscapes then, Troy?" Sutton asked, giving Jake a stern glance.

"I am. I like to find beauty in nature. Trees, mountains, sunsets. It sells well at the local galleries, so I keep it up. I've been thinking about moving into portraits, though," he said as he turned his gaze towards Ellie. "I'd love to talk to you about it more, Ellie. Have you ever done any modeling?"

"I...umm... no," Ellie stammered, shocked at his brazen appraisal of her.

"Dinner smells great, Troy," Jake cut in evenly, arms crossed over his chest and eyes narrowed. "I'd hate to let an empty stomach mar my appraisal of your talents or of you yourself. Shall we?"

Troy pulled his hungry gaze off of Ellie and appeared to see Jake for the first time. "Of course. Where are my manners?"

He turned towards the grand dining room again, a dark, paneled affair. There was a wide live-edge table surrounded by leather chairs. It was trying to be comfortable but came across as sad and stiff.

"Excuse me while I go and tell my staff that we're ready," Troy said casually.

Once he was gone, Jake whistled a low tone. "Well, he is the worst," he said.

"Elle, I'm so sorry! I can't apologize enough. I haven't seen him in years. We mostly just text about sports and stuff. I had no idea that he had become such a jerk. We should go. Let's just go," Sutton said. He was clearly on edge and felt terrible.

"Sutton, it's not your fault. He is a little difficult, but maybe he'll settle down once we get used to each other. Let's give it a bit. He's an old buddy of yours, after all, and you're nothing if not a loyal friend," Ellie said. She smiled at him for good measure, and it seemed to ease some of the tension in his gaze.

"Ok, we'll give it through dinner. If Troy is still acting like this after that, then we'll make our excuses from there."

"Sounds good. The least Troy can do after insulting my sister is offer me a free dinner," Jake said, pulling out one of the large leather chairs. He sat down and put his napkin in his lap, quite at his leisure.

"I'm glad my discomfort has benefited you, Jacob," Ellie said in a sarcastically formal way.

"As am I, Eleanor," Jake said, matching her tone for tone.

"Soups on!" Troy declared as he walked through the swinging door that adjoined the kitchen and dining room.

After they all took their seats, Troy on one side next to Jake with Ellie and Sutton on the other, Dinner was served by a staff of two women. Ellie wondered if they were always here or if Troy had hired them for the evening to impress them all.

"So, Sutton, how's Portlandia?" Troy asked in an overly dramatic tone, waving his fork around between bites.

"It's fine. Work is going well. That's about all I have time for."

"So you aren't dating… what's her name? Katie?" Troy asked, scrunching his face up to remember. Ellie imagined it was difficult for him to remember details about anyone's life besides his own.

"We broke up last spring," Sutton said without emotion.

"That's a shame," Troy said dismissively while he speared a potato. "Ellie, what about you? Are you seeing anyone?"

"Nope," Ellie replied with a small smile and shrug. She hoped that her short answer would close the subject.

"I'm not either, in case anyone was wondering," Jake added. "I'm just taking some time to 'date myself,' really trying to find out who 'Jake' is, you know? Discover what makes this big heart of mine beat."

Troy just turned that blank look on Jake again, but Ellie and Sutton laughed.

"Is that what you call eating alone, Jake?" Ellie asked.

Sutton offered his friendly, quiet chuckle, but Troy, Troy let out what could only be considered a holler of a fake laugh. It was enough to make Ellie jump and drop her fork in a clatter.

"Pretty and funny! You just have it all don't you, Ellie?"

She gave him a sidelong glance and scowled, "I suppose so…"

Sutton watched her reaction and scrambled to jump in. He cleared his throat and said, "So Troy, have you been following the Broncos much this season. They're looking pretty good, huh?"

"Hmm?" Troy said without taking his eyes off of Ellie. "Why don't you ask Ellie? She knows a thing or two about looking good."

"Alright…" Jake said, throwing his napkin on the table. Ellie could tell he was ready to pounce. He put on a show of being an enlightened, peace-loving, liberal thinker, but he wasn't averse to a tussle now and then.

Sutton beat him to the punch. As Jake was pushing his chair out, Sutton knocked his over to stand up. It fell in a soft thud as the leather landed on the thick woven rug. "What are you doing, man?" Sutton said incredulously.

"What do you mean?" Troy replied. He leaned back in his chair lazily, still not taking his eyes off of Ellie. She had stopped feeling uncomfortable under his gaze. Now she just wanted to laugh.

"I can't believe you're hitting on her. Right here in front of us!" Sutton said. Jake had stood up by now, but wasn't saying anything. Instead of speaking, he continued eating while he stood, obviously content to let Sutton step in.

"Oh, I'm sorry man," Troy said with the first hint of self-awareness and remorse they had seen all night. "Am I honing in on your territory here? Do you two have something going on?"

"No!" Ellie and Sutton both said in surprise, immediately dismissing the idea.

"I don't understand then," Troy replied, obviously confused.

"If you're not benefiting from this whole situation, there's no reason I shouldn't."

Sutton was about to respond and, based on the way he crossed his arms, and his green eyes grew three sizes in his face it wasn't going to be kind. Ellie stepped in instead.

"There's a perfectly good reason, Troy. I'm not interested," she said politely. Ellie added a smile for good measure and picked up her fork, ready to resume eating her steak.

He smiled condescendingly as if Ellie was a simple girl who didn't know her own mind. "I'm sure I can get you to reconsider, sweetheart." He reached across the table and grabbed her hand before he winked at her.

Ellie slid her fingers out from under his. "My name is Ellie, not sweetheart, and I don't think you can."

"Come on, man, her brother just died. Show some respect," Sutton said quietly. His tone was cold and threatening, one that Ellie wouldn't want to be directed at her.

"I know. And I'm sure her brother wouldn't want her to be without comfort at a time like this," Troy said with a hint of humor and more than a hint of arrogance in his eyes.

Jake and Sutton held each other's gaze for a split second across the table. They were dumbfounded and furious all at once. Jake pulled his mouth and eyebrows down in a frown before pointing his finger from his chest to Sutton's. "Should we 'rock, paper, scissors' for it?" Jake finally asked.

"Guys, come on…" Ellie said, knowing where their minds were at.

"No, Elle, he deserves it," Sutton said, eyes locked on Jake as they both pounded their fists atop their palms. "Rock, paper, scissors, shoot!" They said in unison.

"What are they doing? What's going on here?" Troy said, a look of confusion on his face.

Ellie rolled her eyes as Sutton and Jake both landed on "rock."

"Come on," Sutton said under his breath.

"Again," Jake said, glancing at Troy, who was still sitting in his chair, brows knit in question.

"I'd leave the room if I were you, Troy," Ellie said on a sigh. "They're trying to decide who gets to punch you."

"Punch me? In my own house? I don't think so. Sutton, you can't blame a man for acting on his impulses. I mean, honestly, how have you not made a move on her?" Troy paused and looked at Ellie again, giving her a once over with his hungry eyes. "With that body? Something must be wrong with you!"

Sutton and Jake paused mid count. "You know what, Jake? I think this idiot has now insulted me and Ellie. Mind if I take this one?" Sutton said.

"By all means, good sir," Jake said, bowing dramatically.

Ellie rolled her eyes for what felt like the hundredth time that evening as Troy jumped out of his seat. The look in Sutton's eyes, coupled with his well-muscled frame, had finally convinced him that he had something to be afraid of.

Troy scrambled on his feet, but Sutton closed the distance in a few short strides. Troy's bravado faded fast as Sutton grabbed him by the collar and leaned in close.

"I don't want to hit you, Troy. We've known each other for a long time, and I'd hate for things to end this way between us. Apologize to my friend, and we'll be on our way."

"Ellie, I'm sorry. Please take my comments as a compliment and nothing more," Troy said softly, hands in the air.

"Good, now apologize for the way you treated her on the ski lift all those years ago," Jake said as he took a sip of his beer.

"Jake," Ellie said in embarrassment.

"No, Elle, he owes you. Sure I've had a good laugh about it all these years. Picturing you dangling from the chair and everything, but he shouldn't have treated you like that. Not after he stuck his tongue down your throat," Jake said. All humor had faded from his face, and his eyes burned with hatred as he stared at Troy over his beer.

"That was you?" Troy said in shock. Sutton still had him by the collar, but he didn't seem afraid anymore. In fact, his eyes got wide, and he started laughing. "That had to have been the funniest thing I've ever seen a girl do!"

"I'm sure," Ellie said under her breath. She was blushing furiously now, her amusement fading fast. They were treading in very uncomfortable waters. Walking deeper and deeper into the roots of her insecurities about dating. She was forgettable. Uninteresting. Good for a laugh and nothing more, and it was all being drug out in front of people she loved at this horrible dinner.

"So you saw it and didn't help her?" Sutton said, his ire rising again.

"Nah," Troy shrugged Sutton's hands off of his collar and sat back down. "Wasn't a good enough kiss to get that involved."

And there it was. What Ellie knew all along. She wasn't good enough. She knew that it was stupid. That all of this took place when she was just a kid, but she also knew, deep down in the hidden, vulnerable places of her heart, that this thought was why she was still alone. This was why no men beyond her father and brothers and yes, Sutton could ever love her, and this was why losing one of them cut so very deep. Ellie couldn't stop her face from holding the heartache she felt. She tried hard not to let the tears spring to her eyes, but they came anyway, and she looked down quickly to hide them.

Sutton saw, though, and with a glance, he caught her heartache and transformed it into a rage of his own. He shook his head slowly and rolled his shoulders as if he was trying to brush the words aside.

"You know what, Troy? I really didn't want to have to do this. I didn't. But it has to be done."

And with that, Sutton pulled his fist back and let it fly. It collided with Troy's perfect face, promising to leave its mark.

Troy was shocked, Jake was laughing, Ellie was mortified. Sutton was fuming.

"Let's go," Sutton growled under his breath.

They all turned to leave as Troy called out behind them. "You'll be hearing from my lawyer, Pierce!"

"I graduated top of my class at Harvard Law, Troy. Do your worst!" Sutton replied without even looking back.

* * *

They made their way to a hotel on the edge of Bozeman. A chain establishment filled with subtle patterns and pallets. Unremarkable in every way. Ellie had tried to cover the bill, racked with guilt over what had happened at Troy's house.

"Come on, guys! Let me pay for our rooms. You'd have a free place to stay if it wasn't for me!" She had said.

Sutton had silently refused, letting the sound of his credit card sliding across the front desk speak for him.

He hadn't said a word since they had left. His emotions, already so on edge after everything with Cully, had simply boiled over. He was angry, remorseful, astounded, and sad. So very sad.

"Sutton," Ellie softly said as he grabbed her suitcase. He aimed to carry it for her if only to show her that chivalry wasn't dead and she didn't deserve to be treated the way she had been. She stilled his motion with a touch of her hand.

"Your hand is swollen. You need to ice it."

"It's fine," Sutton said evenly.

"How about the hot tub then?" Jake said on a shrug. "Sounds nice to me, and it might help your hand feel better."

Ellie nodded, and Sutton simply said, "Fine."

Then he picked up her suitcase and carried it all the way to her door.

* * *

Ellie to the family text: "Just checking in. We're spending the night in Bozeman. On track to be there by Thursday. Love you all."

From Lisa: "Glad to hear it. Everything going ok?"

From Jake: "More or less…"

From Janine: "Explain yourselves."

From Jake: "Sutton had to defend Ellie's honor. A parade in his honor is expected when we arrive."

From Samuel: "What happened, son?"

From Ellie: "Jake is being dramatic. Everything's fine. We're all fine."

From Janine: "Jake, keep going!"

From Jake: "Not much to tell except that Sutton punched a guy, and now he has one less college buddy. He's got plenty to spare, though."

From Peter: "I trust the guy deserved it?"

From Sutton: "He did."

From Jake: "He totally did, Dad. I would have done it myself, but rock beats scissors, you know?"

From Janine: "You two decided who would punch him with Rock, Paper, Scissors? Lisa, it looks like we raised a few idiots. Flipping a coin is much faster!"

From Lisa: "I'm just glad everyone's ok. Everyone is ok right…?"

From Jake: "Not the guy who got punched!"

From Rose: "For Ellie? Cully would have punched him."

From Sutton: "Exactly."

* * *

Sutton sat on the edge of the hot tub, staring at Rose's words on his phone screen while the steam rose up and swirled around him in the cold evening air. He knew she was right. That was why he had done it, wasn't it? Because he knew Cully wouldn't have stood for such a thing. Because Cully always had a hair-trigger, always sought out any adrenaline rush. For better or worse.

It was odd the way that his loss compelled change, action, anger. Sutton was still fuming over what had happened. He hadn't hit anyone since he was in high school, and even then, it was while he was playing hockey. Of course, grief had sent all of them spiraling for the last forty-eight hours but deep inside, he knew that something else altogether had gotten into him.

Ellie had. Well, the look of shame and… what was it? Resignation in her eyes at Troy's insult. She had weathered his tasteless come-ons all night but, the moment that Troy had said that the kiss that they shared wasn't good enough, she had seemed to wither before his eyes.

That composure, that confidence he had marveled at all day had slipped, and he saw the insecure girl she used to be if only for a moment. He had been able to tolerate (albeit poorly) a man catcalling her all evening but insulting her? He couldn't bear it. Couldn't bear seeing her belittled.

Not Ellie. Not the one person in his life who was consistently good and lovely and passionate. Not the girl who had grown into a captivating woman without his even noticing.

Maybe that was why he was so bothered, because he hadn't noticed her until now, and he was ashamed that a man as disgusting as Troy had noticed her first.

He shook his head and dipped his fingers into the water, savoring the warmth on his bruised hand. He didn't like where his thoughts were drifting. He couldn't let himself go there. Not with Ellie and definitely not right now. Things in his life were far too muddled, too fringed in sadness.

He couldn't think about pursuing a woman. Not when his sister was burying her husband.

It was best to just chalk his outburst up to brotherly instincts. Why couldn't he convince himself that was true, though?

Sutton sighed and set his phone down, looking up just in time to see Ellie approaching. She gave him a smile as she drew nearer, and he realized that if he had found it hard to put Ellie out of his mind, it would be nearly impossible to do so after she pulled off her robe, revealing her feminine form in her bathing suit. It hugged her curves in all the right places despite its simple lines.

He swallowed hard as she slipped into the water, and her long brown hair fanned out around her, resting on the water's surface. Why had he never noticed how soft her hair looked?

"You ok, Sutton?" she asked gently, a look of sympathy and concern in her eyes.

"Hmm?" he said, caught off guard by her voice.

"Your hand. Is it ok? I'm just sick over the whole thing! To think you hurt yourself and lost a friend on my account. I could just die!"

"Don't think another thing about it," Sutton said evenly. "I had no business being friends with that guy in the first place. I just wish I would have seen that a long time ago."

"It's not your fault, Sutt. You can't help it. You're loyal to a fault," Ellie told him. She reached out and rubbed his shoulder in a comforting way. The same way she always had, but this time, it gave him goosebumps.

"Yeah, well, hopefully, I'll learn my lesson someday," he said with a self-deprecating smile.

"If you're thinking about Kate, you need to stop. You can't

blame yourself for her anymore," Ellie said softly. She was looking down at the water, watching her hands float in its warmth.

No. Sutton thought to himself with surprise. For the first time in a long time, I'm not thinking about her at all.

When Sutton didn't reply, she looked up, ready to press him, to dive into his break up even further, but he spoke, cutting her off.

"Elle, I'm sorry for how I responded back there. I'm sorry if we embarrassed you."

She laughed, but it came out as nervous and harsh instead of its usual, airy melody. "You guys didn't embarrass me. I was more embarrassed to have Troy confirm what I've been worrying about all these years in front of other people."

"What's that?"

"Well, for starters, that I'm forgettable," she answered with a self-deprecating smile.

"Nonsense. I've known you my whole life. Haven't forgotten you once," Sutton said as he pulled her to him in a side hug. She nestled in, her head resting on his shoulder. It felt comfortable, normal, right.

Ellie laughed. "Well, if not forgettable, then a bad kisser." She looked down and shrugged. Her cheeks were aflame but not from the warm water.

Sutton laughed, shocked at her words. "Elle, that was your first kiss! You didn't know what you were doing. And anyway, with lips as perfect as yours, that simply can't be true."

He looked down at her quickly as she lifted her face towards his, her head still resting on his shoulder. Her wide eyes revealed that she was equally as shocked by his words as he was. Did he just say that? Out loud?

Ellie lifted her hand to her lips unconsciously as if she wanted to touch them, to feel certain that his words were true. The gesture was far too becoming. Far too tempting.

Sutton cleared his throat and dropped her gaze as he lifted his arm off of her shoulder. He racked his brain for something to say to lighten the moment, to ease the awkwardness that made even the steaming water in the hot tub feel chilled. Thankfully, Jake did that for them.

"Sorry to keep you guys waiting," he said as he walked towards them covered in the same hotel robe that Ellie and Sutton had found in their closets. "I forgot my swimming suit."

"You better not be in only your underwear, Jake!" Ellie said, looking at him in annoyance, the moment with Sutton and his comment forgotten for the time being.

"Don't get your dander up, Ellie. I found something else."

He pulled off his robe and what he had on was somehow worse.

"Is that a diaper?" Sutton asked through a grin.

"Trash bag," Jake replied, wagging his eyebrows and smiling as he stepped into the water. The white plastic had been wrapped and ripped and taped and tucked until it resembled something between parachute pants and an adult diaper. It ballooned out around him as he settled down into the water, and then slowly deflated, causing bubbles to rise to the surface.

Ellie and Sutton stared for the shortest of seconds, and then before any of them could think, laughter overtook them.

Long, loud, full-bodied laughter. It rose like the steam that floated in the air, purifying and soothing and good.

Chapter 6

S UTTON AWOKE BEFORE DAWN, INTENT ON CHASING away his fatigue with exercise instead of sleep. The hotel had a small fitness center in the basement, and he wanted to make good use of it.

He walked silently out of the room, easing the door shut so as not to wake up a sleeping Jake. The hall was brightly lit, it's fluorescent light creating a canned sense of daytime and cheer.

It didn't fool Sutton. He knew that outside the falsely lit hallway, the sky was as dark as his mood. He hadn't been able to sleep, again, something that had begun to plague him since he found out that Cully had died. He hadn't had a good night's rest in days, and it was frustrating him. He just couldn't make his mind stop racing long enough to fall asleep.

As soon as his head hit the pillow, guilt and sorrow bombarded him. Relentless memories of every missed opportunity with Cully and the family pelted him, tortured him. His ears rang with the haunting refrain of his excuses to avoid coming home. It was like Tinnitus—incessant, annoying, a relentless ringing that was driving him mad.

If only he had said yes. If only he had gone with Cully on his last climbing trip...

Sutton sighed as he jogged down the stairwell, making quick work of the few flights between his room and the fitness center. His footsteps echoed through the empty corridor, replaced only by the squeal of the door as he pulled it open.

The fitness center was small but clean, filled with a few

stationary bikes and free weights. Sutton was the only one there at this early hour, and he was grateful for the solitude.

He walked over to the weights and picked up one in each hand, the cool of the metal soothing him with its familiarity. He had been working out every morning since his dad bought him a weight set for Christmas his Junior year of high school.

Back then, he had walked out to the garage every morning to find Cully and Jake waiting. They had all been intent on bulking up for the football team and for the girls. Well, in Cully's case, for one girl. Rose. Everything was always for Rose when it came to Cully.

Sutton curled the weights towards his biceps, grimacing as the reps piled on. Grimacing as the memories piled on.

Memories of Cully smiling down at Sutton while he spotted him at the bench press. Memories of the sound of his laughter harmonizing with the ringing of barbells.

Sutton's heart raced, and sweat beaded his brow, but he knew it wasn't from the weights he was lifting. It was Cully. Memories of Cully haunting him again.

Will everything remind me of him? Will everything poke on the pain of missing him? He asked himself.

He dropped the weights with a clang and stalked towards the stationary bike. Perhaps this would be the mindless thing he needed. The emotionless release that he longed for.

Sutton began pedaling, easing into the wheel's ceaseless rotations, easing into the idea that they were spinning without taking him anywhere.

Just like his life had been.

He had been spinning his wheels without making progress. A motionless, exhausting cycle.

Sutton continued to pedal, letting his muscles and lungs burn with the exertion. Fatigue dogged him, pulled on his mind and body like the weights he had been lifting. It dulled his defenses and weakened his resolve. Between the repetitive motions of his legs and the exhaustion, his mind was lulled into a meandering mood.

Sutton thought back on his choices over the last few days. Taking time away from work. Maude. His growing attraction to Ellie. None of it was his usual mode of operation. He never would have left everything on a dime. Never would have embarked on a stupid road trip. Never had thought of Ellie romantically.

He had lost himself, had lost all sense of control.

The odd thing was that he kind of liked it. If everything he had been doing had kept him spinning in place, mired in heartache and regret, maybe this was the way out of the rut he was in. Perhaps he was finally going somewhere new. But where?

Sutton slowed his pace, easing his body out of the exertion. He glanced at his phone resting on the top of the bike and saw that it was late enough for the sun to begin rising, late enough for him to stop hiding from sleep and face the day ahead.

They would leave Bozeman and make their way south towards Rocky Mountain National Park. Make their way home towards the mountains that had claimed Cully. Sighing, Sutton grabbed a nearby towel and wiped the sweat from his brow as his phone buzzed on the bike.

A text message from Rose stretched across the screen. "Are you up?" it read.

Sutton typed back a quick response. "Yes, just finishing a workout. Do you need anything?"

"Can we talk?" she typed back.

Sutton didn't hesitate, simply dialed his sister's number and lifted the phone to his ear. If she needed to talk, he would talk until he was blue in the face.

"Hey Sutt," she said softly. Sutton could hear tears in her voice and it caused his heart to seize and stop.

"Rose, are you ok?"

"No, but I didn't expect to be," she said on a humorless laugh. "Are you ok, Sutton?"

He sighed and rubbed his hand along the back of his neck. Of course, he wasn't ok. He had lost his best friend. He was talking to his widowed sister and floundering for a way to steal her tears away and banish them forever. He couldn't say any of that to Rose, though. Her heartache was far greater than his.

"It doesn't matter how I'm doing, Rose. I want to be here for you, to talk about you," he finally said softly.

Rose sighed. "I don't really have anything to say, Sutton I just couldn't lie here in the bed I've shared with Cully and feel so alone. During the day, I can find things to stay busy with, can pretend that things are normal. I can trick myself into thinking that he's just at work or out of town, you know? But at night, in the early morning hours, he's supposed to be here. I can't trick myself in bed. I can't ignore his empty pillow…"

Rose's words trailed off, and Sutton heard her sniff. He pictured her sitting on her bed, legs curled up under her like she always did, hugging Cully's pillow close to her. The image nearly undid him, and Sutton had to physically fight off the panic rising up within him by throwing his towel hard towards the bike. He had to get her out of that bed, away from Cully's pillow.

Sutton looked deep within himself for composure, for control, for the steadying presence his sister needed.

"Rose, I want you to get out of bed. Can you do that?" he said gently.

She gave him a soft "yes," and then like a child, awaited his instructions.

"Ok, now I want you to walk downstairs and go into the kitchen. You're going to make yourself some coffee. Pour the water and grounds into the coffee maker just like you do every single day."

"Coffee. I can do that," Rose said distractedly. Sutton heard the squeal of her bedroom door, and the slightest sense of relief began to ebb within him.

"I'm in the kitchen, Sutton. I'm making the coffee."

"Ok, great. What are you going to have for breakfast?"

"Breakfast? I don't know… Cully always liked eggs, so I usually make those but…"

"How about some oatmeal, Rose. You like oatmeal," Sutton cut in, through tears. He hated to hear how lost his sister sounded, how devastated. He had to get her into her normal routine. He had to force her to move and live and find the hard and comforting truth that life could go on even without Cully.

"Ok, I'll have oatmeal."

"Great. Now, why don't you water your plants while you wait for it to cook."

Sutton knew that flowers filled Rose's heart with joy. Knew that she had violets resting on her kitchen window sill. He wondered if she had been keeping up with them or if she had been blinded by grief. He couldn't stand the thought of her walking into her kitchen one morning and finding them dead. Finding that the death of her husband had begotten more death.

Sutton heard her turn the water on and he exhaled slowly, hoping that the rote motions brought a sense of normalcy to her heart.

"This is helping Sutton. It's helping to have someone to talk to while I do normal things," she said thinly. "Keep talking."

"Alright," Sutton said gently. He forced a measured tone into his words as he scrambled for something to talk about. "Jake packed all of his stuff for our trip in trash bags."

Rose giggled half-heartedly. "He's a millionaire and still doesn't own a suitcase. Oh, Jake."

"It's alright," Sutton added smiling. "His aesthetic fits with this road trip. You should see the hunk of junk we're driving in."

"I bet it's charming in its own way," Rose said kindly and hoped flagged within Sutton. Rose was an optimist by nature. Always able to see the bright side and defend it. Sutton was glad to see that a little of that lingered despite her devastation.

"If you think that the 1970s were charming, then sure," Sutton replied laughing. "You should have seen Ellie's face when she saw it for the first time."

Rose laughed. "I'm sure she tried to find something endearing about it. Ellie isn't picky."

"No, she's never been critical a day in her life. Her eyes said a different story, though."

"Well, I know for a fact that she would ride in the ugliest, smelliest car in the world if it meant spending time with you. She's missed you so much, Sutton. We all have."

Sutton sighed and sobered at Rose's words. "I know. I've missed you all. What are you doing now, Rose?"

"I'm pouring my coffee. Then I'm going to eat."

"Good," Sutton said in relief. He could hear a change in Rose's voice. She didn't sound so lost, so sad. Realization was creeping in on Sutton, though and it caused fear to fan into flame.

He had never heard Rose sound so despondent, so confused, so aimless. Grief was stealing her capacity. Loneliness had set siege to her mind and heart.

He didn't want her to be alone.

"Rose," Sutton said hesitantly. "I think you should go stay with Mom and Dad for a few days. I don't want you to be alone right now."

Rose sighed. "I know. I don't want to be alone either. I thought it would be better… being near Cully's things. I thought it would be comforting to sleep in our bed, to smell his scent on our sheets…"

"No, Rose," Sutton said fiercely. "You're torturing yourself."

"I know, Sutton. I'll go today, ok?"

Sutton felt the tension go out of his shoulders. She wouldn't be alone and that's all he cared about. She would go home to their parents and let them walk her through the motions of living.

And then, he would step in and do it for them. Sutton hung up with Rose as clarity overtook him. In the span of one phone call, Sutton had found his way out of the rut.

He would find a job in Denver, move in with Rose and fend off her loneliness one day at a time. Sutton would be there for her until she could face the home she had made with Cully on her own.

Chapter 7

THEY WERE TWO HOURS OUTSIDE OF BOZEMAN, AND it was raining. Hard. Hard enough to have lulled Jake into a sound sleep in the back seat while Ellie took her turn as co-pilot. Ellie didn't mind the rain, though. It matched everyone's mood. With the devastation of losing Cully and then the events of yesterday, rain clouds were fitting.

The ache of grief was constant, like an underlying headache threatening to turn into a migraine at any minute. Ellie had never had a migraine before, but Sarah got them from time to time, and they were absolutely debilitating. The usually passionate and caring Sarah couldn't bring herself to so much as lift her feet off of her bed, so incapacitated was she by the pain she carried.

Ellie pictured her friend lying down, eyes closed, sensitive to every sight and sound and smell, and thought how odd it was. The pain only existed in her head, but it transcended every physical limit, reached down into her whole body, out into her whole environment, and stole every bit of comfort from her.

Grief was like a migraine. One point of pain that overtook every part of you and Ellie couldn't let that happen. Not here in this disgusting van with two men that loved her enough to fall apart at the sight of her tears.

She cleared her throat, flipped her hair back behind her shoulders, and grabbed on to any topic she could find. Anything to break the silence and keep the splitting pain at bay.

"Sutton, tell me about your new house. Your mom told us all

that you bought it last February, but I haven't seen any pictures or anything."

Sutton tensed beside her, rolled his neck as if to stretch out a pain.

"I sold it," is all he said without looking at her across the car.

"What? You just bought it! You didn't even give yourself a chance to build any equity," Ellie replied, scowling.

"I didn't need it," Sutton shrugged and looked in the rearview mirror before changing lanes.

"The equity? Must be nice…" Ellie said under her breath with her eyebrows raised.

"The house, I didn't need the house," Sutton cut in, laughing humorlessly.

"Of course you did! You need somewhere to live, Sutton and real estate is always a wise investment. Are you sure you thought this through?"

"I thought through the sale enough. It was the buying that I didn't think through."

"How so?" Ellie asked gently.

"I bought it for Kate," he replied on a sigh as he looked unswervingly on the road ahead. "For Kate and me and the three kids we were going to have in the next six years. Actually, Ellie, I proposed to her in the kitchen of that house, and she turned me down. I tried to keep it, to live there and get over it, but every time I cooked something, all I could think about was the awkward moment when I told her to untie the blindfold around her eyes, she saw me down on one knee, and shook her head no, over and over again. I figured I might as well capitalize on my pain and make a buck or two by selling it."

"Oh, Sutton, I'm so sorry! I didn't know… I wouldn't have pushed… I'm sorry."

"Don't worry, Ellie. I'm over it. Well, I'm over the hurt of it. The anger is still there, but what can you do, you know?"

Ellie nodded, letting the pieces of the last year of Sutton's life fall into place. He had had the rug pulled out from under him. Over and over again.

"Sutton, if it makes you feel any better, I think I read that it's cheaper to rent than buy in Portland. You really did make the best choice."

Sutton gave a humorless laugh, reached across the car, and squeezed Ellie's shoulder. "Always, Mrs. Bright Side, huh?"

She shrugged and smiled. "I just hate that I accidentally keep pushing on your sore spots."

Sutton sighed and shrugged in return. "There have been quite a few lately. Ok, enough about me. Your turn. You haven't said anything about your personal life. What about that guy you were dating last time I saw you? He was nice, wasn't he? Is he who sent you those flowers?"

Sutton floated the question in the air, but his tone was awkward as if he was worried about asking, or perhaps about hearing the answer.

"Greg? We ended things over a year ago," Ellie laughed. "I can't believe you even remember him."

"Well, you brought him home for Thanksgiving the same year that I brought Kate home. Of course, I remember him."

Ellie sighed. "I didn't so much bring him home as he invited himself over for dinner because he was skiing with friends in Colorado that weekend. That's part of why we broke up. He was too presumptuous."

Sutton's eyes sparked as he looked across the car at Ellie, anger had taken hold, and he looked the same way he did right before he punched Troy the day before. Like he was just looking for a reason to explode. Looking for a reason to be reckless and mad. "What do you mean presumptuous? What kind of things did he presume? Did he force you to do anything you didn't want, Ellie? Was he a jerk to you too? God, I should have known with Troy when we were kids, and I should have seen it that Thanksgiving! I was too caught up with keeping Kate happy though… Too lost in my own world to see what was going on around…"

"Sutton!" Ellie cut in, "What has gotten into you? All I said was he was too presumptuous. He invited himself to stuff, ordered my food for me, stuff like that. He was just kind of annoying, not a sexual predator or anything. Your fuse is way too short lately!"

Sutton sighed and rubbed his neck with one hand while keeping the other on the wheel. Thunder cracked in the distance, an exclamation point to the end of Sutton's mood. "I'm sorry, Ellie, I just… I don't know. I'm just mad. About a lot of things."

"I know. I'm sad about a lot of things."

They were quiet for a moment, the sound of Jake's snoring and the rain hitting the roof of the van the only accompaniment to their foul moods. Ellie pondered the events of the last few days, thought about the way that her usually easy-going friend had behaved. There was an edge to him that she hadn't noticed before. A wave of anger hovered below the surface.

Not just that, though. Something else had changed in him. Never before had he been protective of her. He had watched her go off to prom, weather a break-up or two in college, get rejected after her first few auditions, but never had he offered anything more than encouragement and a "you'll get 'em next time" kind of attitude.

It was odd. Not altogether unwelcome but odd all the same.

"Why are you so protective of me all of the sudden, Sutton?" Ellie said. She needed to keep things in the open. Needed to have answers as the questions came. There wasn't any room in her heart or mind for more confusion than she already had.

Sutton seemed caught off guard by her question, unsure of how to answer. Finally, he sighed. "That's a tough question to answer, Elle. I don't know."

"I think you do, but you don't want to. I think you know, but you won't say it."

"What is that supposed to mean?"

"I think you're acting like this because you're upset that Cully isn't here to be my big brother so you think you have to do it. I think you're mad because you can't protect Rose, your actual sister so you're trying to protect me instead. You don't have to, though, Sutton. Don't put that pressure on yourself. I don't want that for you."

* * *

Sutton gazed across the car, dumbstruck by Ellie's comments. She was half right. Had hit part of the nail on the head. She had missed the other half of it, though. She had also failed to see the immense guilt that he carried. The feeling that everything that had gone wrong in the lives of the people he loved was partly because of his absence in their lives over the last few years. The strangling regret he felt over putting his life and his plans in the way of being present in theirs. She hadn't noticed that his outbursts were fueled by a need to never not notice his people again. To never miss a chance to protect them.

She didn't know that Rose's empty arms kept him awake at night.

She had also missed one more piece of the puzzle. His extremely surprising and unwanted attraction to her.

"Sure, maybe," was all he said in response.

Ellie opened her mouth to say something, but the van had other ideas. Sutton felt and heard the tire blow all at once.

"What in the..." he said as he wrestled control of the ancient steering wheel. "This piece of junk can't even get us out of Bozeman without breaking down!"

Sutton forced the van to the side of the road, staring daggers at the storm just beyond the windshield.

Jake still hadn't woken up.

"It's alright, Sutton. Just a flat tire," Ellie said gently. She could see his irritation rising and wanted to combat it.

"Yeah, a flat tire in the rain. Just my luck! Jake! Wake up! You're helping me change this."

"What? What happened?" Jake said groggily from the backseat.

"We got a flat," Sutton growled. "Get out and help me."

Ellie sighed as Sutton and Jake climbed out of the van and crouched down in the rainy ditch they had found themselves in. Rain-soaked through their shirts in a matter of seconds but Jake seemed unfazed as he jacked up the van. Thankfully, the road was deserted filled with nothing but puddles and mud, but Sutton wasn't in any mood to count his blessings.

This trip that he had so carefully planned was supposed to be full of distractions. Happy distractions. Scenery, old friends, adventure, everything Cully would have loved. Everything any one of them would have loved. Instead, they just kept finding themselves out in the rain. Figuratively and literally.

It made sense. At least in Sutton's newly pessimistic mind. Why would he expect anything good to come from such a terrible situation? He began to loosen the lug nuts with a vengeance, releasing his fury and frustration on the metal.

"Take it easy there, Sutton. We're not in any rush," Jake said as he lifted his face towards the falling rain.

"You might not be, but I'm not eager to stay out here in this any longer than I have to," Sutton growled.

"Why?" Jake asked as he helped Sutton lift the flat down. "It's just a little water. We'll dry out."

Sutton ignored his question and rounded the back of the van to retrieve the spare. The vinyl cover that shielded it was cracked and faded from decades of sun. Sutton stood and stared at it, letting the water run down his face, his shoulders, his back, his fingers.

How was it possible that rain or shine, nothing could whether the elements of life? How was it possible that sunshine, happiness, light could wear something down just as much as rain?

Deep hopelessness settled over Sutton. A sense that even if brighter days did come again someday, it wouldn't matter. He was bound to be wet and cold or hot and cracked. Bound to be worn down by life.

Sutton opened his hands flat and pounded on the back door of the hideous van. It rattled and swayed, and the sound that his anger made caused Ellie to jump inside. Sutton heard her let out a tiny, startled scream. He stared at the back of her head, offering a silent apology.

"Look, man, I think this old girl is as ugly and useless as they come, but Maude doesn't deserve a beating. She's still a lady after all," Jake said as he sauntered over to Sutton, hands in his pockets, dark, wet hair falling down over his face.

Sutton looked at Jake, an explanation ready on his lips. He was about to explain the tire cover, how the sun-cracked, faded vinyl had sent him spiraling. How it had looked at him in the middle of this rainstorm and reminded him that nothing gold can stay. How it forced him to see that even bright days left things dried out and useless. How it had felt like someone had handed him a bouquet of bones.

Instead, he decided to let it go and move on with the task at hand. He unzipped the vinyl tire cover and what he found inside caused his heart to sink even further.

"The spare is flat," Sutton said as he ran his hands through his wet hair. The tire was flattened on one side, a nail protruding from it, sticking out like a middle finger and taunting him. "Who puts a flat tire back and leaves it?"

"The last owners must have found themselves in a similar situation to ours and forgot to change the spare out. Tough luck, huh?" Jake offered, shrugging. He fingered the nail as if inspecting the craftsmanship of it, unwilling to meet Sutton's angry gaze.

"I never should have bought this stupid thing," Sutton finally replied, unable to keep a note of defeat from taking his voice captive.

"Nonsense," Jake offered. "She's just high maintenance. I don't mind high maintenance women."

"Well, I've had my fill of them," Sutton said.

The rain was picking up and was no longer a drizzle but a deluge. Lightning crackled in the distance lighting up the dark sky, splitting it in two for only a second. It must have alarmed Ellie for she rolled down her window and yelled to Jake and Sutton to come back inside the van.

With nothing to be done about the tire, for the time being, they obeyed her, yanking open the old doors and throwing themselves inside.

"You don't need to change the tire in a storm like this. Just wait until it passes," she told them eyeing their sopping wet clothes.

"We can't change it anyway," Sutton said. "The spare is flat."

Ellie scowled in frustration. "They sold you a flat tire when you bought this thing? That's not right! They shouldn't have taken advantage of you like that!"

"Being taken advantage of is the least of my worries. I just want to get us a tire and keep moving." He wanted to get home to Rose as soon as possible.

Jake had pulled out his phone by now and was looking up tire shops nearby. They were on a remote stretch of road but were only a mile or so out from the next town. With any luck, they could walk into town and buy a new tire once the storm passed.

Sutton sighed, resigned to the situation. Waiting out a storm—wasn't that just the story of his life.

Chapter 8

AN HOUR HAD PASSED, AND THE RAIN STILL HADN'T relented. It was no longer a deluge, but it was steady and strong enough to keep them tucked inside the van. They attempted to fight off the boredom and frustration by playing catch with a deflated football they had found under the bench seats.

"We can't wait here much longer, we're wasting too much time, and I'm getting hungry," Jake said as he tossed the ball in Sutton's direction.

"Here," Ellie said handing Jake the bag of Sarah's cookies. "There's still some of these left."

Jake pulled one out and then handed the bag around to Ellie and Sutton.

"These are good!" Jake said through bites. "Sarah made these?"

Ellie nodded, smiling at the mention of her friend. "She's an amazing baker. Amazing at everything she does, actually."

"She's gorgeous too," Jake added. "I couldn't keep my eyes off of her when I came to visit you last winter. Knowing what I do about her baking abilities now, I think it's safe to say she's wife material. Tell Sarah that if she ever wants to fall in love, I'm available."

Ellie laughed and rolled her eyes. "You're not her type, Jake."

"I'm every girl's type," he replied, brushing off her comment. "Wealthy, handsome, funny…"

"… and humble too" Sutton cut in, tossing the ball to Jake.

"Exactly," Jake said. "I think I could convince Sarah to go on an adventure with me. Maybe I'll invite her to follow the butterfly migration with Maude and me next year."

Ellie laughed. "You'll have to do a lot better than Maude to convince her to come with you, Jake."

"I don't think so. Sutton convinced you to come along with this old girl. If it worked on you, It'll work on Sarah." Jake picked the football up and started throwing it again. Ellie caught it and threw it towards Sutton.

"Sutton convinced me to go along on this trip because I hadn't seen him in years, and I wanted some quality time with my old friend. I missed him just like the rest of us did," she said with a shrug.

Sutton caught the ball and winced at her words. She hadn't meant to make him feel bad about his absence, she didn't know that he carried more guilt than he could name over it, but still, it stung.

"I'm sorry, Ellie. I'm sorry I was gone for so long.," he said with a sigh.

"It's ok! You're here now," she offered with a simple smile and shrug. She held his gaze and he was struck by her openness and trust. There was a lightness to her demeanor, an ease that came with forgiving easily and seeing the best in people. It was a gift to be seen that way, one that lightened the burden of guilt and regrets that he carried.

"We're all here now," Sutton replied with a smile. "We've been here in this spot for too long. I can't take this sitting still much longer. I think I'll go get the tire."

"It's still raining, Sutton. You'll get soaked all over again," Ellie argued.

"I'll just put on one of Jake's trash bags," Sutton shrugged. He was already rummaging in the back of the van and pulling out a bag.

"Finally, you've come around to my line of thinking!" Jake said.

Ellie laughed, a sound that filled the van with sunshine despite the storm. It was musical and bright, just like the rest of her, powerful in its purity and simplicity. It made Sutton's stomach flip, and he noted the reaction. Noted it and acted on it before he could think.

"Did you really miss me, Ellie?" Sutton asked tugging a trash bag out of the box.

She tilted her head and smiled demurely. "Very much, Sutton."

He threw the trash bag her way and smiled back. "Then come along."

* * *

Ellie's hair was soaked, drenched from the roots to the ends. She didn't mind, though. It had been sweet of Sutton to invite her along, and she wouldn't have dreamt of declining. Not when she could tell that he was trying so hard to make up for lost time. Not when he was so obviously racked with regret and guilt over losing out on the last years of Cully's life.

She was determined to make memories, build relationships, live life even in the rain. So, she walked beside Sutton, gathered the dripping strands of her hair, and pulled them into a loose braid as they went.

"How do you do that so quickly?" Sutton asked, watching her fingers weave the strands together.

"Years of practice, I guess," Ellie said shrugging.

"It looks pretty like that," Sutton told her.

"Thank you," Ellie replied, smiling. It wasn't like Sutton to be so complimentary towards her. He must really feel guilty about ignoring the family for the last few years.

"Sutton, you don't have to be so nice to me," Ellie said, shoving him with her shoulder. Their trash bag ponchos brushed up against each other creating a scratching sound that fit with the soft, percussive rainfall. "I'm not mad at you."

"What?" Sutton asked looking at her in confusion.

"You've been so complimentary and protective of me the last few days and I'm afraid that you feel like you have to prove something, make up for something. Or maybe you need to take Cully's place and be my cheerleader. You don't have to do that."

Sutton nodded, taking his time to answer. "I do feel like I have things to make for, Ellie but that's not why I said that about your hair just now. I meant it. It does look pretty. You look pretty. I just want you to know that."

Ellie looked at him, studying his strong jaw with a few days-worth of growth on it. His muscular frame towered above her as they walked side by side, making her feel small and feminine.

She couldn't help but notice how striking he was, and her mind wandered back in time to the first time she realized how handsome Sutton was. They had been teenagers, and all of them—Cully, Rose, Jake, Pippa, Sutton, and Ellie, were spending a summer afternoon on the Pierce's back porch eating ice cream. The summer sun sent its rays down, warming them all and striking them with that rare combination of contentment and energy that comes with summer-time and adolescence. The air was scented with Roses and vanilla, and the birds had chirped an accompaniment to Ellie's daydreams.

Ellie had glanced over to say something to Sutton, had seen him looking her way with the sun illuminating his green eyes, and something shifted into place in her mind. She had been unexpectedly attracted to him. Had been struck with the knowledge that Sutton Pierce was one of the most handsome boys in the world.

She remembered feeling like Eve in the garden of Eden. Like she had taken a bite of something forbidden at that moment, and because of it, she could never go back to the way things were before. She could never erase the knowledge she had that Sutton was attractive. Of course, she had never told him that she thought so, had never acted on it or even hinted towards it. Sutton being equally as attracted to her was a complete impossibility so why entertain those thoughts?

Still, over the years, the knowledge of her attraction crept up every so often, and this was one of those moments. Ellie pulled her eyes off of Sutton's profile, trying not to think about the fact that he had said she was pretty. He was just being kind. Just trying to build her up like Cully always did.

There was no way he meant it, and it was best to change the subject before her imagination had any more fuel for its fire.

"Did I tell you the theme for the Holiday season at work?" Ellie asked, veering the conversation into safer waters.

Sutton shook his head no, smiling down at her. The rain was finally dying to a misting and the air smelled crisp and clean.

"It's Christmas classics but not classical. I mean all the songs you like, from the '40's you know? 'I'll Be Home For Christmas', 'What are you doing New Years' stuff like that."

"Those are all the best Christmas songs. I'd love to come to one of the performances," Sutton said, completely surprising Ellie.

"Really? You could get away from work for that?"

"Work isn't going to be an issue anymore," Sutton replied. It was an odd thing for him to say, but Ellie didn't push. Not when she might be able to have Sutton come visit at Christmas time.

"Come then! You can stay with Sarah and me, and I'll get you the best seat in the house."

"And I'll take you out for dinner after the show," Sutton said.

Ellie tried to mask her excitement, tried to keep her tone natural and light, but it was hard. Sutton had been distant for so long, and now, here he was making plans to come and visit.

"Alright, Sutton, but if something comes up and you can't come, that's ok. I don't want you to feel any pressure or anything."

"I'll be there, Ellie," he said firmly, decisively. "The weekend before Christmas, I'm coming to Seattle to watch you play all of my favorite Christmas songs, and then we'll go home for Christmas together."

"Ok, then," she replied, smiling. "But Sutton, can we please just fly home this time? I'm not interested in walking two miles to get a tire in the snow."

He laughed and gave her a playful shove. Causing her to laugh in return.

"I love when you laugh, Elle," Sutton said, eyes shining down at her. "It's so lilting and beautiful. It sounds like music."

Ellie's heart skipped a beat at another one of his compliments, and she couldn't help but countdown the days until their Christmas dinner.

Chapter 9

T HE SUN HAD BEGUN ITS DESCENT BY THE TIME JAKE parked Maude in front of the tiny log cabin they had rented in Estes Park for the night. It was small but quaint, with red drapes hanging in the windows and potted yellow mums on either side of the front door. Two stone chimneys stood like bookends on either side of the house, rising upwards, piercing the yellow, purple, and orange sky. They reminded Ellie of torches, holding the flames of light that the sunset created.

She climbed out of the backseat of the van, stretching her weary limbs. They had been driving for ten hours straight, stopping only for gas and meals at fast-food chains along the way to make up for the time they had lost from the tire debacle.

"The key should be in an envelope under the flower pot on the right, Elle. Can you open up the house while we get the bags?" Sutton said from the other side of the van. She couldn't see his face but could tell by the tone of his voice that he was happy to be out of the car and breathing some fresh air.

Ellie walked across the graveled driveway and up the creaky wooden steps. The key was right where it should have been, and she made quick work of opening the door.

A musty, old scent greeted her. It smelled like her childhood and the countless family trips to cabins just like this one scattered around the Rocky Mountains. The Baxters and Pierces always took a summer trip to the mountains together. They were some of the happiest memories that Ellie had from those long-ago days.

The cabin was small but well-appointed, with a tidy kitchen to the right and a hallway that led to two bedrooms and a bathroom just beyond it. The sitting room sat to the left of the door, and it beckoned Ellie to sit and rest. One of the stone fireplaces stood in the middle of the living room wall, it's sides blackened with the soot and memories of fires long died. A couch as old and faded as Maude herself sat under the west-facing window and a rocking chair sidled up next to it. The evening sunset spilled into the room, bathing the faded interior in melting light. Honeyed tones pierced every corner and set the room aglow. Ellie followed the waning sunbeams with her eyes. Like a spotlight, it shone on the opposite wall where a piano stood, begging to serenade the mountain views and cozy hearth. Beckoning to outshine them both with the songs it could ply from heartstrings.

Ellie smiled to herself, knowing she would be able to convince Jake to play for them. Knowing she would love playing right along with him.

As if her thoughts had summoned them, Sutton and Jake crossed the threshold, arms full of suitcases and trash bags.

"Will it suit, Elle?" Sutton asked with a tired smile on his lips.

"It's perfect," Ellie replied.

* * *

An hour later, darkness had fully descended, and night with all of its comfort had enveloped the tiny cabin in the woods. Ellie had found a can of hot chocolate in the cupboard with a note from the cabin's owners to "enjoy" it.

While she boiled water, Sutton got to work making a fire. Jake had claimed the shower upon their arrival and hadn't been seen since.

She wished he would reappear. She needed his easy-going sense of humor to lighten her mood. Without him, there was nothing to do but sit in silence and remember.

Remember what it was like as a kid to stomp through mountain trails with Cully leading the way. Remember how his ghost stories around the campfire left her afraid to sleep at night. Remember how he and Rose had looked on their wedding day at the top of one of these Rocky peaks, Cully in jeans, Rose in white, everyone clothed in joy.

She felt close to Cully here. Like his memory was a fire, and she was standing near enough for its heat to burn.

The memories pelted her in rapid succession. Bringing joy and anguish all at once. Her breath became ragged and strained, and she felt a sense of panic rise up. She had to force her mind to change course, had to think about something else.

"A penny for your thoughts, Sutton," she said to him as she turned and faced him over the kitchen counter. Her voice sounded shrill and thin, and she hoped it didn't give her away.

He looked back at her over his shoulder and shrugged. "Can't say that I have a penny's worth of thoughts at the moment, Elle. My brain is fried."

"Your brain is too smart to be fried. Tell me something. Anything." She sounded desperate and knew it.

"You ok, Ellie?" He asked. His eyes narrowed slightly in concern, the exact reaction Ellie knew he would have but didn't want.

"I'm fine," she said too brightly. "Just ready from some hot chocolate. How about you? How's the fire coming?"

Sutton scowled as flames flickered and cracked to life behind him. He looked at her and tilted his head, ready to say something, but Ellie cut him off instead. She didn't want him prying and forcing her to talk about anything she wasn't ready for.

"I think we should play some music. I need the practice, and you probably do too. What do you say?"

She didn't wait for his response, just crossed the room and sat down quickly at the piano. She began to play scales like her life depended on it, fingers franticly climbing up and down the keys. She didn't even glance at them, it was as natural as typing was for anyone else.

"I'm nowhere near as talented as Jake, but since we can't seem to get him out of that shower, I'll have to do. Any requests?" Ellie said quickly. "Actually, no, let me guess. Jazz. You'll want jazz. How's this?"

Her hands changed position abruptly as she dove into "Don't Get Around Much Anymore."

The syncopated rhythm poured out of her fingers, bouncing off of the keys and filling the room. Ellie scrunched her eyes closed in response. She knew she was playing too stiff, pushing the rhythm faster than it needed to be, but it felt good. It eased the ache ever so slightly.

"Or maybe not that one," she said over her shoulder without stopping. "Maybe you want this one."

She transitioned right into "Our Love is Here to Stay," paying closer attention to the timing, forcing herself to do better with this song. To maintain the right beats per minute.

"Your rhythm is off," Sutton said as he leaned against the mantle, arms crossed, a smirk on his face.

"Don't you start with that, Sutton," Ellie replied, shaking her head. "I know this piece. I've known it for years, and I'm playing it exactly how it's written."

"Can't play Jazz exactly how it's written, Elle."

Ellie stopped playing and rolled her eyes. "I knew you would say that."

"It's cause you know I'm right," Sutton said with a smile and a laugh. "You can't read Jazz you..."

"...have to feel it. I know. I don't want to feel right now, though.

I just want to play what's written. I want to hear and know and do. Not feel." Ellie interjected harshly, painfully.

Sutton's smile froze on his face and then fell, like a flower that bloomed before the last frost.

"I see, Elle. Then forget the Jazz. Just for tonight," he replied, compassion and understanding dripping from his tone like a tonic for her soul.

"No," Ellie said softly. "It's your favorite, and while I don't want to feel, you might. It might be just what you need."

"And what do you need, Ellie?" Sutton asked gently.

"A distraction," she replied with a sigh as she stopped playing. "I don't want to think about how much Cully would have loved this place or how he used to tell me scary ghost stories by the campfire and then hug me while I cried from the fear he caused. I don't want to think about how views like these were the last he saw. I can't…I need to not think about him and when it's silent, he's all I can think about. So if you aren't going to talk to me, this will have to do. You'll have to put up with my overly perfect Jazz playing. You'll have to take it as the selfish gift that it is, ok?" Tears had begun to pool in her eyes, and they threatened to fall. It didn't matter if they did or not. Sutton saw them anyway.

Sutton nodded and, without a word, disappeared down the hall.

Ellie sighed and rested her head on the piano. Had she made him angry again? Before she had any more time to think on it, though, he returned with his guitar in one hand and her violin in the other.

"If it's a distraction you're after, then I think these will suit us a little better."

A smile broke across Ellie's face, and relief bloomed in her heart. "You dear, dear man!" She said as he handed her the violin. He smiled in response and sat down on the couch.

"What are we playing?" Sutton asked

"Really? You're letting me pick? You never let me pick!"

"Well, you better decide quickly before I change my mind then," Sutton said as he pulled his guitar out and began to tune it. His pick rested between his teeth, and Ellie found herself noticing the shape of his lips, the way they moved and rested.

She looked away before the thoughts could take root and forced herself to think about the music.

Ellie took a quick mental inventory. She could call upon the classics. Beethoven or Bach. Sutton wouldn't know them off the top of his head, but he would quickly pick up on the key signature and strum along like he had done when they were teenagers and had filled their summer afternoons making music together. He was a master at improvisation, and his flexibility always amazed her. She knew he would do it for her, but she wanted him to enjoy this as much as she would. She ached to play, to numb the pain with music, but for some inexplicable reason, she ached to please him even more.

To see him smile.

It came to her in a flash.

"Alright, I've got one, but only if you promise to go along with it. Singing and everything," she said with a smile.

Sutton sighed and continued to tune his guitar. She knew he assumed she was going to force him to sing something like "Ave Maria" and wasn't thrilled about it. To his deep, abiding credit, though he said, "Alright, I promise."

She smiled at him, tucked her violin under her chin, and let the bow rest in its place.

She pulled a long, even note and then dove into the opening strains of "Tennessee Whiskey."

Sutton laughed as she massaged vibrato and run after run out of her violin. "Blues, huh? I can play the blues," he said over the music she made.

"Then get to it," Ellie said with a wide smile.

He dove in with her, adding the sounds of his guitar to her violin. The strings wove together, strands that were not easily broken. Strands that created a tapestry of feeling and sound. Ellie and Sutton played the opening refrain, repeating it a few times through, allowing themselves to get lost in the poignant notes. They were entranced, mesmerized by it until suddenly, Ellie dropped out and pointed at Sutton with her bow, cueing him to sing.

It had been years since she had heard him sing a single note. Had been years since they had made music together, but there in the little cabin, it was as if they hadn't missed a beat.

Sutton's deep, textured voice filled the room. Singing of days gone by, of old comforts that had proven empty. Ellie let her bow rest on her lap, let the sound of his voice carry the melody, and cut into parts of her long since gone dark.

His voice sounded like home. Sounded like warmth and days gone by. It's richness climbed and fell nimbly over the notes, taking on runs and nuance effortlessly. Ellie breathed in deeply and closed her eyes, letting the warmth of the moment sweep over her. Letting Sutton ease her weary heart with his song.

* * *

Sutton had forgotten how it felt to create music with Ellie. Had forgotten how well their songs fit together.

It didn't take him long to remember. As soon as he reached the chorus, her gentle, rich voice climbed on top of his, lending harmony to his melody. The sounds they made fit like bricks atop each other, locking in place, and building a sanctuary of sound.

He looked over at her across the room, looked at the woman who was creating this duet, and was struck again by her beauty. Her eyes were closed, and she swayed on the bench, but it was her smile that nearly took his breath away. She looked peaceful. Content. Happy.

And he was responsible for it.

They kept on playing. Kept on singing. Kept on filling the room with their song, hanging each note like pictures on the wall, like something beautiful and precious that decorated the moment.

It hemmed them in, this sound. Covered them, warmed them, sheltered them. Sutton had forgotten the refuge that music could build. Had forgotten how it felt to build it with Ellie.

His mind wandered back in time to when they were younger. When they were but teenagers sitting in the sun-soaked music room at the front of the Baxter's house. Their days were filled with summer jobs, chores, sleepovers with friends, but somehow, most days, they always ended up there.

Sutton and Ellie always, the others most of the time.

They took turns suggesting new songs to perfect. Ellie always suggested classical, forcing Beethoven's "Moonlight Sonata or Bach's Violin Partita No. 2 in D Minor" on them all. Their complexity had frustrated Sutton, but he had eventually mastered them all, much to Ellie's delight.

In return, he forced Sinatra on her. Every last hit. He had always given her a hard time about the stiff way she played jazz, something that caused her to memorize every piece he offered if only to prove her perfection and passion for the music.

He had always given her a hard time, but he never meant it. She had mastered each and every one.

While they threw out their own versions of classics, Jake and the rest would sprinkle in popular covers, and just like that, the days passed in musical bliss.

They had all loved it, but Ellie had been the only one to build a life from it. To take the tapestry they had woven together and wrap herself in it, define herself with it.

Sutton knew there at that moment, as he watched her fall into a trance within the music that she was the only one worthy of it.

While she could get lost in the song, he could get lost in watching her within it.

And Sutton would have if it wasn't for Jake.

"You guys started without me?" He said as he entered the room. His hair was wet, and he was wearing sweat pants and a white t-shirt.

Ellie paused playing and Sutton followed her lead.

"Here," she said, rising from the piano bench. "You take over here. We were just warming up."

Ellie smiled at Jake as he sat down at the piano. She crossed the room and joined Sutton on the worn couch, her small frame barely disturbing the cushions. Sutton immediately sensed her nearness, and something stirred within him.

What was going on? This was Ellie. The woman who was like a sister to him. Or at least had been. Until yesterday when something had cracked and bloomed in him all at once. He glanced over at Ellie, who was laughing at something that Jake had said. What had it been? Sutton had missed it completely. He had been too busy noticing her. Noticing how her presence made him feel.

You're not thinking clearly, he told himself silently. *You're exhausted and reeling from everything that's gone on. You're in no place to fall for any woman, let alone Ellie. Not after everything with Kate and especially not right now. Not with Cully dead and Rose grieving. Get a grip.*

But he couldn't. Not with Ellie laughing and singing next to him. Not with her head tilted to the side just enough that he could smell her shampoo, see the firelight reflect off of the dark, shiny strands of her hair. He needed to get up, to leave. Needed to put some distance between them. This flame that had been lit didn't need fanning. It needed drenching.

Now.

"Actually, if you're done in the shower, Jake, I think I'll take a turn," Sutton said as he rose stiffly from the couch.

"Alright, come back when you're done. We're just getting started," Ellie said, smiling up at him from the couch. She was completely oblivious to the sway she suddenly held over him. All the more reason for him to leave the room.

"I'll probably just turn in, Ellie," Sutton answered, looking away from her so he didn't see the inevitable disappointment in her eyes.

"Already? Are you feeling ok?" Ellie said with concern in her voice.

"I'm fine," Sutton replied while he tucked his guitar back in its case. "Just tired."

"Fine, we'll just have to play without you. It's probably for the best anyway, Sutt. You'll just hold us back," Jake said as he dove in on the piano.

"Now that's not true, and you know it, Jake. Sutton is the best guitarist I've ever heard," Ellie shot back, scowling.

Jake just pounded the keys louder, though. Ignoring Ellie's kind protests. She rolled her eyes, looked over at Sutton, and shrugged before she started playing with Jake.

"Goodnight, Sutton!" She yelled over the song. "Oh, and thank you. For the distraction."

He nodded and gave her a half-hearted smile as he turned down the hall.

The distraction. That was the perfect way to put it. Ellie Baxter had distracted him completely, and he didn't know if he was strong enough to avoid it.

Chapter 10

OLD AIR WOKE ELLIE AROUND MIDNIGHT, SNEAKING into her bedroom through the drafty windows and reminding her that autumn nights in the Rocky Mountains weren't much different than those in the winter. Her pillow felt wet, and she realized she had been crying. It was no wonder. She had been dreaming of Cully. Dreaming that she was sitting by him at the dinner table, but no matter what she said, he couldn't hear her. She had yelled and cried herself hoarse, but still, he just sat there, as still as a statue, as unapproachable as a ghost. Ellie's heart clenched at the memory, at the fact that her nightmare was too close to reality for comfort.

She shivered under her covers, trying to warm herself and quiet her heart all at once. It seemed an impossible task. Grief was unavoidable. It found her even in her dreams, and she felt trapped by it.

The cold seemed a small problem in comparison to that, but even still, it was one problem she could remedy. Ellie glanced across the room at the dark fireplace in the corner. She smiled in relief, imagining the cozy feeling the flames would bring, the warmth and the comfort that she would feel falling back to sleep by firelight. It was enough motivation for her to reluctantly slide out of bed and walk across the cold floorboards towards the hearth.

The room was dark save for the light of the moon, but her eyes were adjusted to the murky blackness, and she was confident that she could find her way around. Her confidence was one thing. Reality was another. Before she took more than three steps, Ellie collided with a footstool, the one that she had completely forgotten about between her bed and the fireplace.

Ellie stumbled and reached out to steady herself, an action that only made matters worse. Her hand, in search of the dresser, found everything on top of it instead and sent a decorative box and lamp clattering to the floor. She flinched at the racket as the bedroom light suddenly flickered on.

Ellie froze, turning her gaze towards the doorway, embarrassed to have been caught in such a clumsy situation.

"Ellie, are you ok?" Sutton's voice came from the doorway of her bedroom. He was wearing sweats and a t-shirt, and his hair was tousled from his pillow. Ellie had an unexpected desire to reach out and tame it, to run her fingers through the brown strands and let them linger for only a moment.

"I'm fine, I was just walking over to light a fire in the fireplace and tripped," she replied, trying to squelch the thoughts that she was having.

Sutton looked at the mess on the floor and then back at Ellie, trying not to laugh. She could only imagine how comical she looked, hair messy, lamp cord tangled at her feet. "Why were you doing that in the dark?"

"I don't know, I just wanted to get it done as quickly as I could and get back under the covers. It's freezing in here!" Ellie replied on a shiver. "I'm sorry I woke you."

"I wasn't asleep, just reading in bed," Sutton replied with a smile and a shrug.

"Well, then I'm sorry to take you away from your book."

"It's no problem! Why don't I light the fire, and you can untangle yourself from that mess."

Ellie nodded her thanks while Sutton crossed the room and found a box of matches on the mantel. He struck one, and it filled the room with a hiss and a flash. Ellie watched his back as he bent over and gently blew on the flame, coaxing its gentle whisper into a mighty, roaring blaze. Warmth began to fill the room, and Ellie smiled.

"There, that should do it," Sutton said leaning back on his heels and flashing a handsome smile Ellie's way. She couldn't deny that he looked striking by firelight, his green eyes and dark hair catching the glow of the flames. It did something funny to Ellie's stomach, seeing him there like that.

"Much better! Thank you!" Ellie smiled her thanks, hoping her thoughts didn't show.

Sutton stood to leave, but for some reason, Ellie didn't want him to. She remembered her nightmare, recalled how it felt to sit there in an echo chamber of grief and loss. She didn't want to be alone. Her heart was heavy, the fire beautiful, and neither thing should be faced alone.

"Sutton, would you stay for a minute?" Ellie said softly. She grabbed the comforter off of the bed and draped it around herself as she sat down on the floor in front of the fire.

"Stay?" Sutton asked as he turned from the doorway.

"Just keep me company for a little while. I don't want to be alone. When I'm alone, I get too sad," Ellie answered. She looked at him with pleading eyes and knew she sounded vulnerable, weak. It didn't matter, though. Sutton wouldn't think less of her.

He nodded and sat down by her on the woven rug near the fire, resting his arms on his knees.

"Thank you, Sutton. I promise I won't make you stay long. I'm sure you're tired."

He shrugged. "I'm happy to stay with you, Ellie. I can't sleep anyway. That's why I was reading."

"Is your book good?"

"Not really. This is better," Sutton answered, sending her a smile.

"The fire?" Ellie asked.

"No, being with you."

Ellie looked over at him expecting to see a lighthearted grin on his face. Instead, she saw something different. There was nothing lighthearted in his eyes at all. They were intense and full of desire, smoldering like the flames before her. He had never looked at her like that before. No one had ever looked at her like that before.

Perhaps it was the firelight, or maybe it was the late hour, but something felt clear and right in that moment. She felt safe and warm under Sutton's gaze. Known and comforted and treasured. He meant it. He wanted to stay right there with her. He didn't want to be anywhere else. But why?

"What's wrong, Ellie?" His voice was tender and curious, full of care and concern. He must have read the confusion in her eyes, followed the tracks that the tears had left on her cheeks.

"I had a dream. About Cully. It sounds so childish now that I say it out loud, but I'm afraid to go back to sleep. I don't want to dream," Ellie gently tossed her words into the fire, offering them as kindling.

Sutton nodded and followed her gaze. "I know what you mean. My problem isn't dreams, though. My problem is quieting my mind enough to go to sleep. I can't stop thinking about him. About how I should have been there with him that day that he fell."

"I'm glad you weren't there," Ellie said in surprise, a scowl creasing her brow.

"Why?" Sutton asked, matching her tone.

"If you had been there, you would have been forced to live with the image of him falling to his death for the rest of your life. It would have ruined you, Sutton. It would have eaten you up inside until nothing was left," Ellie reached over to him and rubbed his shoulder, trying to instill confidence and comfort. "You weren't meant to be there, Sutton. You weren't meant to carry that with you."

"Maybe not, but I'm carrying a lot of guilt instead. This wasn't the only thing I missed out on with him, with everyone. I've been absent for a long time now, pursuing a life I don't even enjoy, and for what?" Sutton said. His voice was laced with such sadness, such regret, and Ellie longed to erase it. Longed to make him know how proud she was of him. How proud they all were.

"Sutton, the life you've built is worthwhile! You've found such success! I'm so proud of you! There's no place for guilt here. You are good and honorable, and there's no one else I would rather have sitting with me right now." Ellie forced fire into her eyes, conviction that she needed Sutton to feel. Yes, he had been absent, but she had never faulted him for it. Didn't he know that she was in his corner? That she wanted nothing but joy for him?

Sutton pulled her towards him, and she rested her head on his shoulder. He placed his arm over her as they leaned back against the bed, finding comfort in each other as much as in the trappings of the room.

Ellie felt hemmed in. Safe. Sutton's hand on her arm, his shoulder cradling her head, his solid frame next to her, sent her nerve endings to flight. She had been close to him before, had been held by him before, but it had never felt any different than when Jake or Cully touched her. It had never caused her heart to race.

But something had shifted over the last few days. Something had shifted in him over the past months. There was a deep sadness, a loss, and it seemed that he was looking to her for comfort. He was looking to her as much as she was looking to him.

Ellie searched her heart, scared of what she was found there. She was enjoying this. Relishing Sutton's touch, glowing under his gaze.

Stop it, Ellie. She chided herself silently. He's just being a good friend. He's only here because you asked him to be.

At the thought, embarrassment flooded through her. What was she doing forcing Sutton to sit here with her in the middle of the night? The realization that they were in her bedroom, sharing firelight and blankets sent heat racing up into her cheeks. This was romantic. Too romantic. What must Sutton think of her?

Suddenly, she wrenched her head off of his shoulder, filled with a need to end the moment, to explain herself. "We should get to sleep! It's so late. I've monopolized you for far too long."

"I told you, Ellie, I can't sleep. I'd rather stay here with you. You're not monopolizing me."

"I startled you out of bed and then forced you to stay here with me in the middle of the night."

"I'm glad you did," he said softly. She looked at him, and his eyes held desire again. Their green depths were filled with tenderness and sincerity.

He reached out to her, pulling her close, gently cupping her head and laying it down on his broad shoulders again. He rested his cheek on top of her head, and Ellie couldn't stop herself, couldn't pull away a second time. Sutton reached out with his free hand and clasped hers, squeezing it like he had done when they watched the sunset, and her heart began to race anew.

"Stay here with me, Ellie. I'm finally here, with you, and I don't want it to end."

She knew she should get up, knew she should put some distance between them. She couldn't, though. Sutton felt too good, too comfortable, and she surrendered to the confusing weightlessness she found while resting on his shoulder.

* * *

Sutton looked down at Ellie while she slept on his shoulder. She had drifted off a few moments before, and he didn't want to disturb her. Her chest rose and fell in silent breaths, and he prayed that her sleep was as peaceful as it looked.

The fire sent light and shadow in equal parts across the panes of her face, causing her features to glow like embers. Sutton was mesmerized, thankful for the light, and the way it afforded him a chance to stare at her. How had he never noticed how breathtaking she was? How had he missed her graceful curves, her delicate lines, her beauty?

His eyes roamed from her face to her form, studying the curve of her waist, the length of her legs, the fullness of her lips. With each glance, he became more and more aware of her weight against him as she slept on his shoulder.

He was entranced.

It wasn't just her beauty that had captivated him, though. It was her heart. He had forgotten how big it was. How deeply she felt and how freely she offered comfort and encouragement. She offered grace too. Deep, abounding, endless grace. He had soaked up every last word she had offered, and it had been a balm to his guilt-riddled mind. As he sat with her head resting on his shoulder, Sutton thought that perhaps he had soaked up enough of her grace to offer it to himself.

Maybe she was right. Maybe, just maybe he could stop blaming himself for so much and move forward with his life.

Sutton took a deep breath. It had been so long since he had been around a woman as good as Ellie, and there was a thirsty place deep in his soul that was crying out for more of her.

So much for avoiding distraction, Sutton, he chided himself silently.

He had never intended to put himself in such a tempting situation. He had genuinely thought that he would just check on her and leave, but when she had looked at him with her wide, sad, beautiful eyes and asked him to stay, he couldn't say no.

And between the firelight and her touch and her comfort, he couldn't leave.

Ellie took a deep breath and exhaled softly on a sigh, a sound that reached into his heart and pulled every string imaginable. Before he could stop himself, he turned his face towards her hair and let his lips rest in the soft strands, let himself give in to the desire to kiss her, even if it was just the top of her head. Her hair felt like silk under his lips, and he could only imagine that her lips would feel even softer.

This is Ellie, He told himself in an effort to shake some reality into his thoughts and emotions. *Ellie Baxter that you're fawning over... maybe you should have done this a long time ago.*

The reality of how right she felt in his arms was getting harder and harder to deny. Even still, it would be wise not to act on impulse, wise not to pursue her without a little more thought. He needed to leave before he did something he regretted. Needed to get away from the firelight and beauty that filled the room.

"Ellie," he whispered softly while he gently squeezed her shoulder to wake her. "Ellie, you should get in bed. It's late."

"Hmm?" she said, still half asleep. Her voice was gentle and sweet, veiled in sleep, and trust. The sound pulled down the last of his defenses, stoking the warmth and tenderness that had blossomed within his chest. Ellie blinked the sleep out of her eyes and smiled up at Sutton.

"Let's get you in bed," Sutton repeated gently, hating that he was ending the moment.

She stretched and yawned, sleep lingering in her eyes and tinging her with such vulnerability that he wanted to pull her close and hold her longer. Instead, Sutton stood slowly, helping her up off of the floor.

As if Ellie read his thoughts, though, she stood and fell into his arms, squeezing him in an embrace.

"Sutton, thank you for sitting up with me. I know I should be stronger, but the sadness, it sneaks up on me sometimes, and I'm glad you were here," she said as she rested her cheek on his chest. He held her close, breathing in the scent of her hair again. It was intoxicating, like the finest of wines that chased away any inhibitions he had.

"Ellie…" he said softly. He knew his tone gave him away, knew that it held too much longing, too much care, and the look in Ellie's eyes as she pulled her head off of his chest and looked at him said that she knew it too.

"Yes, Sutton," she asked breathlessly.

The hope and anticipation in her voice nearly undid him, nearly pushed his heart over the edge and into her hands, but, at the last minute, he reined himself in.

"Goodnight," he said softly, and with one more look, he let her go and walked towards the door.

Chapter 11

T HE MORNING DAWNED CRISP AND BRIGHT, AND ELLIE greeted it with a contented sigh from the front porch. Its freshness was beguiling. It's newness promising. Despite all the sorrow that awaited her, she would be going home in only a few short hours. Going home to her mother and father and the rest of the people she loved more than life itself. But Cully wouldn't be there, and that was enough to weight every joy and pull it down to earth.

Home without Cully was as bittersweet as the coffee in her hands. As comforting and as scalding as a thought could be. Ellie pinched her eyes closed and kept the tears from falling, kept them locked up inside, and slowly, the feeling passed.

Ellie set her sights on the view in front of her, gazing at the fall leaves and Rocky mountain peaks. It was breathtaking, perfect, captivating in every way, but even with her eyes fixed on such perfection, her mind wandered to Sutton.

As if summoned by her thoughts, Sutton pushed open the front door, arms full of luggage. Ellie smiled at him, blushing as she glanced at his face in the light of day.

"Good morning, Sutton. I made some coffee inside if you want any," Ellie said brightly, as he walked towards her.

He set the bags down by Maude and smiled back at her. "Thanks, Elle. I saw it."

He held her gaze a beat longer, seemed like he was going to say something more but instead, he just stared. At her. Silence fell then. All-around and Ellie felt her pulse pick up and urged her to fill the quiet air. "Well, I'll go and grab my bag, then."

"Jake's getting it," Sutton replied as he fiddled with the keys in his hands.

"You guys talking about me?" Jake's voice came from behind Ellie, and she turned to see him walking out of the cabin, her suitcase and his trash bag in hand. "All good things I'm sure," he said as he winked at Ellie.

"We're ready to go then?" Ellie said as she watched them load up. "You don't want to enjoy the mountain air? Go for a walk?"

Sutton shut the back doors of the van, tucking their luggage inside the brown monstrosity. "I'd rather just get home, Ellie. I know none of us are too eager to face the emotions of it all, but there's no use prolonging the inevitable."

"I guess you're right," Ellie sighed. "I'll just go put this mug in the kitchen, and we can go."

She did just as she said, returning to the front porch a few minutes later. But the scene she found was different than the one she had left.

Sutton and Jake both stood behind Maude's open hatch, revealing a steaming engine. Sutton furiously stared at the van's inner workings while Jake rested one hand on his hip and the other on Sutton's shoulder.

"She needs a jump, buddy," Jake said. "That or a new engine. It could possibly be the transmission or the timing belt too. I've heard starters are real trouble makers in automobiles. Perhaps that's what it is. A bad starter. Or maybe it's the oil. Maybe the oil isn't sitting right with the Old Girl. More oil? New oil? Less oil? Different oil? Who's to say, really."

"Look at us, talking about her like she's not even here," Jake added. He leaned down and put his ear towards the engine. "Maude, feel free to chime in anytime. We're listening, sweetheart."

"Shut up, Jake. You don't know anything about cars," Sutton laughed as he shoved Jake. He sighed heavily, running his hands through his dark hair, something he always did when he was frustrated and grasping for composure.

"I know that those are all possible diagnoses for a car," Jake said with eyebrows raised. "I know that the more options you list, the more likely you are to be right. It's simple laws of probability, Sutton." Jake tapped his head with his finger. "You know I'm right… about something," he added with a sheepish shrug.

Sutton slammed the hatch shut and pushed Jake's hand off of his shoulder. "You're something, alright. And so is this piece of junk. Can't even get it to start," Sutton said as he dug in his pocket for his phone.

"Great. No service. How are we supposed to get a tow to a mechanic?"

"There's a landline in the house," Ellie offered. "I think I saw a phone book too."

"A landline and a phone book? Great!" Jake said with sarcastic enthusiasm. "1992 called, and it's here to save the day! I'll go and make a call."

He walked up to Ellie on his way into the house. "I'll take care of the van, Elle. You see if you can do something about that mood Sutton's in," Jake said under his breath. He gave her a low whistle and raised his eyebrows, accentuating his comments. Ellie laughed and batted him on the shoulder as he went in.

She looked at Sutton. He was leaning against the car, looking out at the mountains stoically. The anger and sadness that had been close at hand the whole trip had descended on him again. She knew that it was a product of their circumstances. Knew that it was the same enemy threatening her, but she would try to help him all the same. She closed the distance between them and leaned against the van next to Sutton.

"There are worse places to be stranded, huh?" Ellie asked as she gave him a little shove with her shoulder.

Sutton didn't reply, just smiled down at her sadly.

"It's just a minor setback, Sutton. We'll be on the road in no time."

"Every part of this trip has been one setback after another. We should have just flown home," Sutton said. He picked up a rock and threw it off into the distance. They watched it soar and then land in obscurity off in the distance.

"Why didn't we just fly, Sutton?" Ellie asked.

"Guilt mostly," Sutton replied, shrugging. "On the night that I found out that Cully had died, I saw this ugly thing sitting there abandoned and for sale. Cully had always talked about getting a camper van and going on the perfect road trip. I thought this was my last chance to honor him, to feel closer to him, to make up for lost time and the adventures we would never have. I wanted to do something that Cully would have done."

Ellie nodded her understanding. "I see where your head was at, but If Cully had been in charge of this trip, we wouldn't have had a route planned, wouldn't have had places to stay lined up, we just would have driven until we wanted to stop and slept on the cold, hard ground. And he would have somehow made it enjoyable. Despite all of the setbacks, you did an excellent job planning everything. If it wasn't for your poor choice in college friends… and vehicles, it would have been completely uneventful. You were trying to be like Cully, but this was a Sutton road trip through and through."

She looked up at Sutton, smiling at him, hoping that her words brought him some sort of comfort. Hoping he felt known and accepted and validated.

"A Sutton trip. Yeah," he replied under his breath. "One where people I care about are left stranded. Where the best-laid plans always fail."

"Sutton, that's not what I meant," Ellie scowled.

"I know that's not what you meant, Elle. You're far too kind to say or mean that. You only see the best in people. You never see their faults," Sutton said on a sigh.

"I'm not being kind, Sutton just being honest. That's what friends are for, right?"

"Maybe I don't want you to be my friend, Ellie," he said softly.

"What?" she whispered, confused.

"Not anymore. I want…" His eyes flicked down to her lips and lingered there. Suddenly everything that was fuzzy became clear. The way he had looked at her over the past days, the comments he had made, the awkwardness that had lingered between them at times.

Sutton had feelings for her. She had suspected that something had blossomed in both of their hearts, tiny buds of hope and beauty, but now it was obvious that those feelings had actually exploded. A riot of emotion and care that she hadn't known they could share.

She studied his eyes, saw the longing and hurt that lingered there. Ellie imagined what it would be like to let Sutton hold her. To let him comfort her and to comfort him in return. To weather the storm of grief they were about to face together. The thought settled into her heart, and she was surprised to discover how well it fit.

But there was something else in his eyes too. A recklessness. Desperate anger and sadness. And Ellie knew that she couldn't give him what he needed. She knew that she wanted to. That she wanted him, but their time hadn't come yet. Maybe it never would.

Love built on grief was too great a risk, too unsteady.

"Sutton," she whispered. "You don't know what you're saying. We can't do this. Not now. Not like this."

"Why not, Ellie?" he asked softly. He pulled her towards him, ever so gently, and she went, unable to stop the desire she had to be held by him despite her reservations. He wrapped his arms around her and hugged her to him. His strong arms encircled her, pressing her ear to his chest, forcing her to hear it beat out his plea.

"Why can't we just be right here for a moment. Get lost in the moment and forget about everything else?" He said gently, longingly.

"Because you're right. You'll let me down, and I'll let you down. We're too broken right now. This won't be what you want it to be, Sutton. I'm not good enough to fill that aching place inside you. You'll see that eventually, and then where will that leave us?"

His arms fell from around her, leaving her feeling cold and abandoned.

"You're wrong, Ellie. You're more than good enough. I think you're the only good thing I've ever known, and I need you. I need you to fix this… this ache inside me. I need your goodness, Ellie, or I'll never get out of this pit that I'm in."

Tears fell freely from her eyes now, tears for this man that was so broken and beaten. Tears for herself because she felt the same. And tears because she knew that she cared for him, wanted to be the one to heal him, but couldn't.

"Oh, Sutton," she finally said, lifting her hands to his face. "I can't be the one to fix you. I'm not strong enough or good enough to do that."

"You are Ellie," Sutton said. His eyes looked fierce, full of conviction and longing. He reached his hands up to hers, and brought them down, held them tight. "You are strong and beautiful and passionate. You're everything I've ever needed, and I don't know why I didn't see it before now."

Sutton let go of her hand and reached up to stroke her face. He wiped her tears with his thumb, a gesture that nearly cracked her heart open. "You're the most beautiful woman I've ever known," he whispered. He leaned down and brushed his lips against hers. His kiss was soft yet desperate, passionate yet timid, and Ellie was swept up in it. "Please, Ellie…" he said as he kissed her again. "Please."

Ellie didn't know what to think. Sutton's kiss felt more perfect than she ever imagined it would be. She could see herself getting lost in it. Doing exactly what he said. Forgetting everything else and just being there in that moment. She wanted nothing more than that. But warning bells clamored within her mind, and panic began to rise up.

She couldn't do this with Sutton. Couldn't dive into a relationship. She knew how these things went. Knew that any man that had ever been with her had eventually realized she wasn't what they wanted, wasn't enough to make them happy. She couldn't risk that happening with Sutton. He was too important to her, meant too much.

Romance only ended in loss, and she had lost one too many people she loved already. She couldn't lose Sutton too.

"Stop!" she gasped, pulling away from his lips. "Please." Her words sounded strangled by the panic that had wrapped its fingers around her throat. She raised her hand to her forehead, an unconscious attempt to still her racing thoughts, to grab ahold of the reins and force them to remain steady. She was ashamed to see that her hands were shaking.

"Ellie, I'm sorry…" Sutton said, alarmed. "I didn't mean to force anything. I thought…"

"No, it's alright, Sutton. I just… I can't do this. Not with you.." She choked out. "I'm sorry." She turned her face away from him, desperate to find some composure, but none came fast.

Sutton reached out and brushed her shoulder with his hand, tenderness and heartache pouring from his emerald eyes. Ellie longed to lean into his touch, but she knew she couldn't give in. Not now that she realized how Sutton felt and the risk that she would be taking. So, instead, she backed up another step and shook her head, silently stopping him.

"Ok, Elle," he whispered, letting his hands fall to his side. "I'll leave you alone."

Ellie looked at him, tears still falling freely. She held his gaze for another breath, hoping he saw how much it hurt her to reject him, hoping he understood the turmoil within her.

She looked at Sutton, her oldest friend, and her heart cracked in two. She was hurting him, pushing him away, but she knew it was for the best.

Ellie saw in herself a desire to be with Sutton forever or not at all. And no matter how tender his kiss, no matter how sincere his desire, she knew forever wasn't something he would want with her. She reached out, grabbed his hand, and squeezed it, hoping the simple gesture conveyed that she was sorry, that she loved him, that she wished she was enough for him.

She let go of his hand, and with that, she walked towards the house and let her tears fall freely.

Chapter 12

SUTTON FELT SICK AS THE TOW TRUCK PARKED IN front of his childhood home. Roiling nausea had been present within him every last mile of the drive home.

"Well, it's been nice getting to know you folks," the driver said. He and Jake had kept up a steady stream of conversation the entire drive, leaving Sutton and Ellie to stew silently in the backseat.

She had barely looked at him since their kiss. Had barely acknowledged him, and even now, she stared out the window, her back turned on Sutton. He could see her sad eyes reflected in the window, though. Could see that they were red-rimmed and anxious.

"Yeah, man let me give you my number so we can hang out next time I pass through Estes," Jake said. The two men exchanged information while Sutton climbed out of the truck. Normally, he was as eager and open to making new friends as Jake was, but today he couldn't force himself to talk. He had spoken far too much of his mind for one day, and it had landed him nowhere.

Sutton stepped out into the autumn sunshine, taking notice of all that hadn't changed in the neighborhood. The lawns still held the green grass of summer and were littered with colorful leaves here and there. In a week or so there would be enough to rake, but for now, they rested on the grass, death, and life dwelling together in sickening harmony.

His parent's house—a brick colonial—stood steady and strong, beckoning him inside. He pictured the entryway, with its brass chandelier and wooden coatrack, pictured the oak table that anchored the kitchen and the striped wallpaper of his father's study. The trappings of his childhood would surround him in only a matter of moments yet he wasn't a child any longer.

He could no longer stand inside those walls and look out the windows at the world with optimism and wonder. He could no longer fool himself into thinking that his life would be as rosy as the bricks that held his memories.

And what of the people he had shared them with? What of the characters that graced every last one?

Cully was dead. And Ellie? What was her place now? How would she look at him? Where did they go from here?

He wanted to erase it all. Every last thing he had said and done. Not because he didn't mean it. He did. He hadn't known he meant any of it until he said it, but once the words had flown out of his mouth, he knew they were the truth.

He cared for Ellie. He needed her. And he had failed to convince her of it.

Ellie's words echoed in his head. "I can't do this. Not with you."

She got out of the car and passed by him silently, leaving the lingering scent of her perfume behind her. Raspberries. She smelled like raspberries. Sweet and fresh and bright. She was walking down the sidewalk towards her parent's home next door, and Sutton saw his opportunity to make things right between them slipping through his fingers.

He cleared his throat and, before he could stop himself, called out to her. "Ellie, wait."

She turned, surprised to hear him say her name, but she stopped, waited for him to say what he needed to. Sutton walked towards her, hands in his pocket.

"I'm sorry," he said quietly.

"For what?" she asked gently.

What was he sorry for? Not for kissing her. He would never be sorry for that. Not for being honest with her. He had meant it even if she didn't believe him. No, he was sorry for hurting her, for making her feel pressured and used. For trying to claim her heart when it was broken and bruised, for trying to claim it without earning it.

He chose his words carefully. "I'm sorry that things happened the way they did. Can you forgive me?"

She nodded her head. "There's nothing to forgive, Sutton. Let's just forget it, ok?"

"I don't want you to forget it," he said.

"Why?" her eyes were guarded. She was worried about what he would say next.

"Because I won't forget it. I won't forget kissing you and how right it felt, and I won't forget hurting you and how awful it felt. I promise I'll do better. I promise I'll show you that I care about you."

Ellie sighed and shook her head. "I need to get inside, Sutton. I'll see you at dinner." Her tone was tired and sad. Defeated, and Sutton's heart fell even farther.

He watched her walk away, wondering how he had somehow managed to make things worse.

* * *

"Sutton, would you go check on the chicken?" Sutton's mother, Janine, said as he entered the kitchen. He had just finished unpacking his suitcase in his childhood bedroom and had made his way downstairs to see what help he could offer.

"Sure mom," he said.

He walked out to the back patio and opened the lid of the grill. His mother had two whole chickens cooking, their juices dripping down onto the grate and sizzling. The meat smelled delicious, and Sutton's stomach growled in anticipation despite the dread he felt about the evening ahead.

In just under an hour, the Baxters would walk over for dinner.

Ellie's mother, Lisa, would have at least three desserts in hand, all perfectly baked and filled with comfort and love. She would set them down on the table while Sutton's mother opened bottles of wine to pair with the meal. They would all hug and tease and smile. The house would be filled with laughter and stories of times long past. Questions about things yet to come. Everyone would sit down at the sturdy, well-worn oak table, the one that had held their food and memories for years, and they would be filled. Filled with food and family and each other.

The two families had done this at least once a week for well over two decades, and it felt like a holiday every time. All the people, all the food, all the comfort of home, but this time would be different.

It would be their first family meal without Cully. The first time his chair would sit empty. It would be a strange kind of torture to experience something so familiar and so unfamiliar all at once.

And then there was Ellie. Sutton would have to see Ellie. Have to endure her presence and beauty while she held him at arm's length.

Sutton sighed and walked back into the house.

"Chicken looks great, Mom," he said as he opened the refrigerator and pulled out a beer. If the night was going to be anything like he assumed it would be, this would be the first of many. For everyone.

Janine stirred the gravy she was making and eyed her son across the room.

"Pre-gaming, huh?"

Sutton raised his brows and took a long drink from his bottle. "I need a little liquid courage to face the sight of Rose sitting at the table next to an empty chair."

Janine nodded. "She's not come out of her room in a while. Maybe you should bring her one of those, give her a little liquid courage so she can make it to the empty chair."

"That's not a bad idea," Sutton said. He opened the refrigerator and pulled a bottle out for Rose.

"Give me one of those too, will you?" Janine said. "I don't think I'm ready for all of this either."

Sutton handed the bottle to his mother, the woman who's smile had been as unchanging as an evergreen throughout his whole life. "Are you going to be ok, mom?" he asked her.

"Not today, but someday I will be. Someday we'll all be ok again, love." She raised her bottle and waited for him to do the same. "Here's to someday."

They clinked their bottles together and then drank deeply of their contents. Someday. It was a hopeful thought.

* * *

Sutton knocked on Rose's bedroom door, pushing it open at the sound of her soft, "Come in."

His sister had always been soft-spoken, gentle, as delicate and intricate as lace. She fit her name. Beautiful and elegant, soft and tender and worthy of adoration. He loved her deeply and steeled himself for the state he would find her in.

"Brought you something," Sutton offered as he pushed open the door. She sat on her bed, cross-legged and smiling softly.

"Ahh, a little pick me up," She patted the space on the bed next to her. "The drink is nice, but my little brother is what I really need. How are you, Sutton?"

He sat down beside her and pulled her into a hug. "Better now that I see your smile. How are you holding up?"

She took a long drink and sighed. "I don't really know. I feel like I'm floating. Like I'm not really here, you know? I feel like none of this is real."

"I wish it wasn't."

"It is, though," Rose sighed. "I'm a widow, and I need to get used to it."

Sutton winced at her words and squeezed her tighter. "Do you need to say that word? Widow? It sounds so harsh. So sad. It doesn't fit you."

"I'll have to make it fit me, Sutt. I'll have to find a way for it to fit me."

"Well…" Sutton said.

Rose sighed and echoed him. "Well…"

She lifted her beer to his and clinked them together. "Drink up, Sutton. It's what Cully would have wanted us to do."

Sutton took another long drink, forcing the beer to push the lump of tears back down his throat. He wouldn't cry in front of Rose.

"So, tell me about that hunk of junk you drove home," Rose said with forced brightness in her voice.

"Don't talk about Maude like that," Sutton replied with a wink. "She's my new girl, and even though she has done nothing but let me down all week, I love her very much."

Rose laughed, a sound that caused some of the tension in Sutton's stomach to ease. "I see you still have terrible taste in women," she teased. "First that Kate and now an old run-down broad."

Sutton didn't say anything, just nodded his head and drained the last of his beer. If his sister only knew the extent of his poor romantic choices lately.

"Not all of us are as lucky as Cully in the romance department," Sutton said.

"I was the lucky one," Rose replied. "Even with him gone, I'm still the lucky one."

Sutton grew silent and pulled his sister's head onto his shoulder. She rested it there, and he saw her tears fall and land in dark puddles on her jeans. He wished he had something more to say, something more to comfort her with, but his hands were empty.

He was helpless, useless, powerless against her grief, and it infuriated him. How could he sit here and do nothing for her? How could he simply hold her while she fell apart?

Guilt and grief and fury crowded in on Sutton. They climbed onto the bed and held him captive. He should be able to fix this, but instead, all he was doing was making things worse. For Rose, For Ellie. For everyone. The urge to do something, to help in some way overtook him. He had to get out of this room, or his anger would overtake him.

"Rose, I forgot I needed to submit a brief before close of business. Excuse me," he said suddenly. It was a lie, of course, but Rose didn't question him. No, he wouldn't be submitting a brief. He would be tendering his resignation.

Taking the first step in helping Rose put the pieces of her broken heart back together. He would focus on that. Not on work, not on his regrets, and not on Ellie.

Chapter 13

A CACOPHONY OF COMFORT ROSE UP AROUND ELLIE, and she inhaled deeply, letting herself soak it all in. Despite their unspeakable loss, they had finally all gathered. All the people that meant home and family to her.

Mrs. Pierce, as Ellie had called her all of her life, had outdone herself as always. The table groaned under the weight of smoked chicken, mashed potatoes, roasted vegetables, homemade rolls, and baked cinnamon apples. Ellie could have been filled up with the smell alone. Every bite burst with flavor, and she wanted to eat until morning. She knew to pace herself, though. Her mother's desserts—pumpkin pie, triple chocolate cake, and raspberry almond shortbread awaited them at the end of the meal.

Both women had done what they always did. Gathered their people with the scent of their food. Comforted their people with the works of their hands and hearts.

Now, with all of them seated at the long table in the Pierce's comfortable dining room, they feasted on the food and company like the starved people that they were.

Voices rose and fell, half a dozen different conversations taking flight and bouncing off of the walls. It tasted like home. Sounded like home. But the feeling that Ellie experienced was too nuanced to be contained in that word. Home.

To be sure, the trappings were the same. The tastes and smells. Even most of the company, but something had shifted. Grief had come and filled Cully's empty chair, and everyone was too nervous to acknowledge it. Too broken to look it in the eye and say, "Well, I suppose you belong here now."

Ellie looked down at the other end of the table at her mother. Lisa Baxter was as unassuming as a butterfly. Gentle and quiet and never one to ask for help. Unassuming didn't mean she didn't have needs, though. Ellie imagined she had needs aplenty sitting there without her firstborn.

"How are you liking this semester, Sweetheart? Ever since you told me about the course load that your thesis is going to require, I haven't been able to stop worrying about you. It's not right to put so much pressure on a young person. Even if it is for education," Ellie's mother Lisa said to Pippa. She could see the heartbreak, the hollow ache in her eyes but, there her mother sat, talking to Sutton's sister Pippa like nothing had changed.

She was ever the mother to anyone who would let her mother them.

"I'm fine, Mrs. Baxter, really," Pippa replied as she picked up her wine glass. "I've been keeping up with the research, and when things get on top of me, I go for a run and clear my head. It'll all be over in a few months anyway."

"I don't know how you do it all, dear. Keep that perfect figure and get the grades that you get. You certainly are blessed," Lisa said. "I could never handle that stress and be as trim as you are. Not in a million years."

Ellie saw her mother eye the cinnamon apples on her plate and then scoop a large yet ladylike bite into her mouth. Lisa had been brought up on the idea that sugar cured all heartache. Ellie's grandmother had reinforced that with every rounded edge of her person, creating a cushion for her family to land with her baking and her body.

Lisa hadn't inherited her mother's physique quite yet but had been looking over her shoulder for it for the better part of her adult life. Especially after she had given birth to her three children and then raised them on the comforts of her kitchen. Sugar was her mother's comfort, and Ellie knew that she would need it more than ever over the coming weeks.

She made a mental note to go to the store in the morning and restock all of her mother's baking supplies.

Ellie took a bite of her potatoes and turned her attention towards her father. He had Sutton engaged in conversation, and Ellie's heart tripped over itself as she watched Sutton nod and smile at something her father said. His green eyes sparkled with humor as he replied to Ellie's father, and they both laughed heartily at whatever Sutton had said. Ellie stared at his lips as they curled up into a smile, watched as they relaxed.

Had she really kissed those lips earlier that day? Had she really rejected them?

She sighed, trying not to let herself second guess her choices. Of course, she had enjoyed kissing Sutton Pierce. Had enjoyed it far too much. But the risk was too great.

She needed to think about something else, needed to stop staring at him.

She turned towards Sutton's father and smiled at him. "Mr. Pierce, how are you holding up, sir?" She asked gently.

The kind older man had always been like a second father to her. Full of an uncommon gentleness and selflessness. He was always most content in moments just like these. With his family and dearest friends surrounding him.

"Ellie, I've told you before, you're old enough to drop the Mr. and just call me Samuel. You're a grown woman and a wonderful one at that," he said as he smiled back at her before taking a sip of wine.

"I know you've said so, sir, but I can't bring myself to do it. Every time I try, I picture the look of disappointment on my father's face and expect a lecture about disrespecting my elders to be forthcoming." Ellie smiled and looked down at her fork.

"Your father is my best friend in the world, but he holds a little too strongly to convention at times. I suppose his army days are to blame. If you'll try to drop the misters and the sirs, though I promise not to tell him."

"I'll do my best. My question still stands, though. How are you holding up?" Ellie reached over and squeezed his hand, reassuring him that she was ready to listen.

Samuel sighed as he glanced down the table at Rose. His eyes filled with tears, and he didn't try to hide them. He was a man that loved his family deeply and never tried to tuck away any evidence that his heart was moved by their plight.

"Ellie, when I walked my Rose down the aisle towards your brother, I didn't have any hesitations. I didn't dread giving her away to him. On the contrary, I looked ahead towards their future together with great joy and anticipation. I dreamt of the grandchildren they would give me, of the life they would build, and how happy I would feel watching them do it all together."

He paused and took another drink. His eyes, identical to Sutton's, turned towards her, and Ellie saw her own anguish mirrored within them. "What I didn't picture was any of this. I didn't picture grieving him." He took a deep, long breath in and then exhaled slowly. "You asked how I'm holding up, Ellie. I don't know that that's the right question. I think what we should be asking is not how we're holding up because that implies maintaining something. Maintaining the thing that we already built. Trying to prop the rubble of our lives back up on the same foundation. But you see, Ellie, we can't do that l now, can we? The life we built and the life we dreamt of are changed now. The foundation has been shaken and uprooted, and we can't hold it up anymore. It's gone."

"Instead, we should ask ourselves this: How are we cleaning up the rubble, and how are we rebuilding? Because that's what we must do. We must build new dreams, new visions of the future using the things that Cully has left behind."

Samuel squeezed Ellie's hand and offered her a small smile, waiting for her to digest what he said. Waiting to offer his patience and grace as she did.

"Clean up and rebuild, huh? That seems like a lofty task. I don't know if I can do that," Ellie replied.

"You can, Ellie. You're strong enough," Samuel said casually like it was a foregone conclusion.

"Sutton said I was strong earlier today too," Ellie said with a self-deprecating laugh. "Somehow, I've managed to fool you both."

"Sutton is a smart man, Ellie. He doesn't say things he doesn't know to be true."

Ellie looked up at Samuel with skepticism in her eyes. She wondered if he knew everything else that Sutton had said. If he was trying to fight his son's battles for him and convince her to give him another chance. She didn't dare question this kind man, though. She would never challenge or confront Samuel Pierce. It would be like arguing with Santa Claus.

"Excuse me, everyone," Rose cut in from the end of the table. "I'm so sorry to interrupt, but while we're all here, I thought it would be best to get a few funeral preparations out of the way."

Ellie's stomach plummeted to the floor at the mention of the word "funeral." Rose seemed unfazed, though. Like she was ready and willing to lay all of the anguish and sadness out on the table. Like she was ready to serve it up with dessert and coffee.

The table grew silent, and all eyes turned towards her. Ellie stared at the woman that had captivated her brother and was struck for the millionth time by her grace and beauty.

Rose held their gazes and offered a small smile. "Mom, Dad," she said, looking towards her ain laws, "I hope I'm not overstepping my bounds in taking the lead on this. You loved Cully first, after all, so please speak up if I am." She waited for their reply with openness and love in her eyes.

"Not at all, Rose," Lisa Baxter replied. Her voice was choked with tears, but her eyes held Rose's. "We'll gladly follow your lead."

"Yes, Rose. I think I speak for everyone at this table, that whatever you want, you'll have. Your family is here, and we'll get through this together," Ellie's father, Peter added.

The table alighted with nods and murmurs of affirmation, like candles flickering to light, the room felt warmed and brightened by the presence of so many willing to offer their love.

"Thank you all. Well, I've been thinking a lot about this. It's all I've been able to think about really, and I've decided that I don't think Cully would have wanted a traditional funeral service. He would have thought it was boring and stuffy. Two things that he never was."

Everyone laughed gently, agreeing with Rose's assessment.

"I think Cully would have been happier with something else. I think he would have liked us all to go to the mountains. Play some music, tell every last story about him, sit by the fire, laugh, maybe cry, and then be done with it. I think he would have wanted us to be together and to make a memory. So that's what I want to do. I want to be together in the place that he loved best and feel and make music and then start to heal."

Ellie looked around the table and saw peace in everyone's eyes. Saw that not a single person disagreed with Rose. This woman. She had loved Cully well and had known him best. Ellie was grateful down to her bones.

Silence fell. Not an awkward silence but a pensive one. Memories of Cully were palpable. Memories of how he laughed as easily as everyone else breaths. How he walked with purpose and ease all at once. Memories of how his voice sounded on a song.

Memories of how his brown eyes caught the sun and how it felt to be pulled into one of his bear hugs.

Of how he came alive when he breathed the same fresh air as those he loved most.

Ellie inhaled deeply, knowing Rose's plan was the only real way to honor the life of her brother.

"I think it's a spectacular plan," Pippa finally said. "Cully would have loved it."

"Well done, my girl," Lisa added, raising her glass of wine towards her daughter. "Well done."

Chapter 14

ELLIE FELT HER TEARS THREATEN AGAIN. THEY were poking at the backs of her eyes like needles that wouldn't be ignored, but she still wasn't ready to let them fall freely. Not here in front of everyone. She wouldn't be the one to break first. Not when Rose was handling everything with such composure.

Thankfully, the conversation had picked back up. With a clear objective in mind, it seemed that the table had been reinvigorated. Rose was laying out all that needed to be done. The cremation. Renting cabins. Planning for food. The music she wanted. Ellie knew it would all fall into place easily. This army of people would fight to the end to honor Cully with everything they had.

She didn't share their exuberance, though. The thought of having tasks to accomplish didn't offer her the distraction she hoped it would. Instead, she just felt exhausted. Fatigue soaked her to the bone, and she knew it was because he wasn't here. Cully wasn't here to offer his energy and love and confidence as a gift.

The heaviness and exhaustion threatened to take over. To pull her eyelids down and lock them shut. She needed to do something. To force her body to move. To remember that she was still alive and could carry on even when life veered off course.

She got up silently and walked towards the kitchen, intent on serving her mother's desserts.

* * *

The kitchen was quiet. Blissfully quiet. The only sound the distant conversation from the dining room down the hall. She set to work uncovering the cake her mother had baked, letting the scent of chocolate invade the room.

Next, she uncovered the pumpkin pie and the homemade whipped cream, taking time to help herself to a taste of the cloud-like treat.

It was lighter than air, and she savored the taste and texture on her tongue. Vanilla. Sugar. Cream. Perfection.

"Hey, quit stealing the whipped cream, Elle. Save some for the rest of us," Jake's voice came from behind her.

"I'm just sampling it," Ellie said.

"That's what I thought you'd be up to. That's why I followed you in here. I've seen you 'sample' it before, Elle, and when you're done, there's hardly any left for the rest of us," Jake said with arms crossed. "You and whipped cream can't be left unsupervised."

"And what makes you qualified to be my supervisor, huh, Jake?" Ellie teased as she pulled a spoon out of the drawer and filled it with whipped cream.

"Well, nothing. I just wanted to make sure I got some whipped cream, that's all. Give me one of those," he said, pointing to the spoons.

Ellie did as he asked and pushed the bowl towards him. He helped himself to a generous scoop and shoved the whole thing in his mouth.

"Remember when we were little, and we would crowd around the counter to watch mom make this stuff?" Jake asked Ellie.

"Yeah, I always thought it was magic. The way the liquid cream could be beaten into a solid."

"It's pretty cool," Jake said. He tried to dip his spoon back into the bowl of whipped cream, and Ellie slapped his hand away.

"No double-dipping, Jake!"

"Fine, give me a new spoon."

Ellie rolled her eyes but complied, getting one for herself too. What could one more spoonful hurt?

"Anyway," Jake said. "I've been thinking a lot about that cream, about how mom beats it into this fluffy stuff. I think there's something to that. Something about life."

Ellie looked at her brother with curiosity. He had always been this way. One minute ridiculous, the next insightful. There was a depth of wisdom within him that was unending and, at times, difficult to access. When he found it, though, he never hesitated to offer it.

Ellie pulled out a third spoon for both of them, scooped Jake more whipped cream, and handed it to him. A silent gesture encouraging him to keep going.

"Something about how life beats us up, but at the end of it all, we'll come out better. Lighter. More solid," he continued.

Ellie held her brother's gaze and smiled at him. He was right. They could be like whipped cream. They could be whipped and beaten and tossed and turned, but at the end of it all, they would come out changed. Solid.

Ellie opened her mouth to reply to Jake, to thank him, but he cut her off.

"Anyway, I gotta go to the bathroom. See ya, Elle."

Oh, Jake. She could never pin him down, and she loved him all the more for it. He walked out of the kitchen and Ellie forced herself to stop eating the whipped cream. She should be getting dessert plated.

Turning towards the cabinets, she pulled down Mrs. Pierce's dessert plates. They were a mismatched collection that she had accumulated over the years. Never one for perfection, Mrs. Pierce had set about building her inventory based on the people who would be eating off of them. She had picked up a floral plate for Ellie's mom

25 years ago. Its rim was trimmed in tiny forget-me-nots, and they wove a delicate, beautiful pattern that Mrs. Pierce had said, "was the essence of her unforgettable and delicate friend, Lisa A Baxter."

Then there was Jake's plate. At least his current plate. He had broken a few over the years, but Janine simply bought him a new one each time, unfazed by his clumsiness. The current model had little red airplanes all over it. Probably because Janine thought that Jake would never grow up, and she didn't want him to either.

Ellie's plate was one that Mrs. Pierce had found at a garage sale when Ellie was ten years old and infatuated with old movies. It had a picture of Audrey Hepburn from Breakfast At Tiffany's on it. Janine had told Ellie that it was because "You and Audrey are classics, my dear. Beautiful, irreplaceable classics."

Ellie smiled at the memory as she pulled down the rest, leaving Cully's (a plate covered in roses) alone in the cabinet. She gathered the stack and brought them over to the counter by the desserts, lost in thought.

She began to sing quietly while she sliced the cake, content. Content until she looked up and saw Sutton walking into the kitchen, making a beeline for the refrigerator.

She didn't say anything, hoping to avoid another awkward conversation.

"No need to stop singing on my account," Sutton said without looking at her. He was staring into the open refrigerator looking for the milk.

"Here's your dessert, Sutton," she replied, grabbing for his plate, (a white plate with his four-year-old handprint smeared in blue paint on it.)

"Thank you," he said quietly. He walked over to her, retrieved a fork from the drawer, and then leaned against the counter and began eating. "Good cake," he said between bites.

"Mmhmm," Ellie mumbled in reply. He was standing a foot

away from her and his presence was making her pulse accelerate and her mind race.

"You're missing out on all the planning in there," Sutton offered, obviously trying to ease the awkwardness.

"Someone needed to serve dessert. Rose can fill me in later," Ellie replied stiffly. She refused to look over at Sutton, refused to hold his gaze and melt in it. "Please don't feel like you need to keep me company in here, Sutton. I'm sure you'd rather sit down and eat with everyone."

"No, this is just fine, Ellie," he said. She could feel his eyes on her. Could feel his desire to mend things. She didn't reply.

He sighed and set his plate down on the counter. "Ellie, is this how it's going to be between us?"

"I don't know what you mean."

"Yes, you do. You won't look at me. You're barely giving me one-word answers. It's awkward, and you know it," Sutton replied gently. "If I had known that this was how it was going to be between us, I never would have…"

"I need to get these on the table," Ellie said, breaking the intense moment. "Excuse me."

She turned away from him and gathered a plate in each hand, but his voice stopped her.

"Rose wants us to do the music. She wants us to play a whole list of songs, all of Cully's favorites. Together."

Ellie froze, letting the realization of what they had to do sink in. They would do it, of course. For Rose and for Cully, but it would require them to push past their awkwardness, and make something beautiful and special.

Ellie sighed, forcing resolve into her tone. "Fine," she said softly. "We can do that."

Chapter 15

S UTTON STOOD IN HIS PARENT'S DRIVEWAY, WAVING as the tow truck hauled Maude off to the nearest repair shop. He had graduated law school with top honors and had managed to build himself a thriving career, but none of those things were any help to him when it came to repairing cars. That was well outside of his area of expertise, and he was smart enough to know when to cut his losses and bring someone else in to do the job.

The mechanic said that Maude's air cooling engine was working too hard, said that he needed to install a fan to give her a little help. That was fine with Sutton so long as he could do it quickly. They were leaving for the mountains in two days and needed Maude to get them there. He couldn't say goodbye to Cully without knowing that he did right. Without bringing the embodiment of his memory along.

Sutton turned back towards the house, intent on grabbing his guitar and walking next door. He and Ellie planned to re-hearse the music for the memorial. Rose had sat down with the two of them the night before and pulled a neatly folded piece of paper out of her pocket. She handed it to Ellie with tears in her eyes.

"This is the list of songs I want to be played. It's a lot, I know, but he loved music. Especially when you two played it."

Ellie unfolded it, read it, and then silently handed it to Sutton.

"It's songs from the first mix CD he ever made me, songs

from his rock climbing playlist, songs from our wedding, you know, Cully's songs. Do you think you can make it happen?" Rose said cautiously.

Ellie reached out and grabbed Rose's hands, squeezed them in her own, and nodded. It was a silent exchange, filled with tears instead of words, but, Sutton knew that these two women could communicate just as effectively that way. That they both possessed hearts that had a depth that only love and emotions could carve. There, in that small moment, deep cried out to deep. And they answered each other with their tears.

It had taken every ounce of self-control Sutton had not to pull Ellie into his arms. Not to wipe her tears and speak comfort into her ear. She had made it clear that she didn't want that from him, though. Not now.

He could still do something about the other woman in the room, though. He could still comfort his sister and give her what she wanted. An answer.

"Of course," Sutton said, walking over to Rose and pulling her into a hug. "Of course."

Now, they would have to make good on their promise.

Sutton walked into the Baxter's home without knocking like he always did. The sunny entryway greeted him with its morning light and blue-flowered wallpaper. The layout of the Baxter's house was similar to the Pierce's, constructed by the same builders thirty years before. The décor was as different as night and day, though.

Where Sutton's mother had a laid back, unintentional style characterized by family pictures and simple décor, Lisa Baxter had gone to great pains to make their home feel like a sanctuary. It was peaceful and calm, feminine in every way.

Floral wallpaper and detailed artwork adorned nearly every room, causing the house to feel like a garden. Having been away from it for so long, Sutton was caught off guard by how it felt to walk inside. Caught off guard by the way that dated and utterly traditional décor could feel so comfortable and peaceful. It was only because of Lisa. It was her calming, gentle, and sweet presence that made the home feel like a place of rest. Her essence lingered in every room, and it felt like an embrace.

"Sutton, dear, come in!" Lisa called as she walked towards him, arms opened wide. She pulled him into an embrace, punctuating it with an extra squeeze before she let go.

"Hi, Mama B," Sutton said, employing his old nickname for her. "What do I smell this morning?"

"Blueberry muffins. Peter and Jake took half the batch with them before they left for their errands this morning. I caught them before they robbed you of your helping, though. Come have a few," she said, leading him towards the kitchen. "I couldn't have you kids playing on an empty stomach, although Ellie already has been. She's been up since six this morning working on her music for work. I told her it wasn't good for her to work so hard before breakfast. I read in Good Housekeeping that it's not healthy for you to do anything that requires much energy before eating a balanced breakfast. It was a lovely article with the most informative graphics with all kinds of statistics. Very colorful. I saved it for you, of course, since I know how you care about breakfast and also your physical health. Let me just find it for you, dear."

She opened one of the white kitchen cabinets and pulled out a folder with Sutton's name written on it. It was the same folder she had been keeping for him since he was in high school. It had started as a place for her to save pages and pages of scholarship applications she had printed out for him for college. No one had asked her to, but everyone had appreciated it.

"You're so very smart, Sutton. We'll get you through Harvard for a song if it's the last thing I do," she had told him.

And she had.

Now, years later, she still kept that folder but filled it with newspaper clippings and magazine articles she thought he might enjoy. Today's stack included the Good Housekeeping article along with one from the Harvard Business Journal and a few reviews of Portland restaurants.

"What would I do without you, Mama B?" Sutton replied, kissing her on the cheek.

"It's nothing, dear now eat up!"

Sutton happily did what he was told, relishing his favorite morning treat.

"Now, Ellie should be down any moment, she's just finishing her hair. I told her it looked lovely without the extra fuss, but she didn't listen. Said something like 'Look good, feel good.'"

"Is she not feeling good this morning?" Sutton asked, trying to keep his tone as neutral as possible.

"I'm fine," Ellie said as she strode breezily into the kitchen, violin, and bow in hand. She had a tight smile pasted on her lips, and her eyes looked tired.

Sutton eyed her across the kitchen, taking in every last detail of her face and form. The morning sunlight caught the golden flecks in her brown eyes and made them shine like treasure hidden in the ground.

"Ellie, sit down. Have a muffin. Your mom said you've been up for hours already. Why not rest for a while?" Sutton said gently as he pulled out the chair next to him.

Ellie shook her head and laid her instrument on the table. "No, I'm fine. We should really get to work rehearsing. I have a few other things I need to do today."

"Like what, dear?" her mother asked.

"I need to get to the store for you, Mom. I noticed that you're running low on baking supplies and I don't want you to be without," Ellie answered. She still hadn't sat down next to Sutton. Still hadn't looked him in the eye.

"Oh, I'll go do that!" Lisa replied enthusiastically. "I'd like to get out of the house anyway. It will be good for me."

"No, don't go, Mom!" Ellie blurted out. "Then we'll be alone!"

"No, you won't, you'll have each other, dear. Now, why don't I just gather my purse, and I'll be out of your hair." Mrs. Baxter bustled about the kitchen retrieving her coupons, purse, keys, and coat, all the while mumbling under her breath about the various items she would purchase at the store. "Flour…five pounds probably… can't forget the vanilla… where's that coupon for chocolate chips, ah there it is… Alright, dears. Don't work too hard. This doesn't need to be perfect. It'll be lovely no matter what. Love you! Be back soon!"

And with that, she flitted out the door.

Ellie cleared her throat. Scarlet circles appeared on each of her cheeks, signaling her embarrassment. She didn't want to be alone with him. He had made her so uncomfortable that she didn't want to be alone with him.

The thought saddened Sutton to no end. This was not the result he had hoped for. He hadn't meant to push her away. He needed to backtrack, make things feel normal between them again. Disarm her.

"Maude should be fine. The mechanic just needs to install a bigger fan to keep the engine from overheating. It'll be done by this afternoon," Sutton said as he brushed his hand over some crumbs on the table.

"Good! That's good news!" Ellie replied with an awkward brightness in her tone.

"Yeah," Sutton answered, smiling.

The silence enveloped them again, heavy and awkward.

"Did you get enough to eat?" Ellie finally asked.

"Yeah, I did. You sure you don't want anything?" Sutton eyed her across the kitchen, trying to read her. She was relaxing ever so slightly. Small talk had its advantages, he supposed.

"I don't have much of an appetite today. Thank you, though," Ellie said. "I'm still full from dinner last night."

"It was delicious, wasn't it?" Sutton said.

Ellie nodded and smiled.

Then, the silence. Again.

Sutton heard the clock ticking on the kitchen wall, heard a few birds chirping outside. He heard everything except Ellie's voice. Suddenly, her phone rang, vibrating and chiming on the kitchen table between them. Ellie and Sutton glanced down at it in unison. Sutton saw the name "Trace" shine up at him before Ellie snatched it up and answered.

A smile filled her face, and a beautiful blush painted her cheeks as she answered. She stood and mouthed, "Be right back," before walking out of the kitchen into the other room.

Sutton watched her go, entranced by her form as she walked. It did odd things to his stomach, stirring the attraction that he couldn't seem to ignore. Something else roiled within his gut, though, too. Jealousy.

Trace was undoubtedly a man. Probably the same man that had sent her flowers and had called throughout their road trip, and, based on the way Ellie smiled when he called, he was probably the man that had a hold of her heart.

Sutton tried not to listen in to her conversation in the other room, tried to feign disinterest, but the melodic and joyful sound of her voice was like salt in a wound. This man was why she had turned him down.

"Sorry about that, Sutton. I just needed to take that call," Ellie said breezily as she came back into the room.

"Who was it?" Sutton asked, trying not to sound upset.

"Oh, just someone I know from work," Ellie said, not looking him in the eye.

Sutton simply nodded, inwardly eyeing the newest hurdle towards winning her heart.

"Should we start practicing?" Ellie asked, a forced brightness in her tone.

"Ellie, wait. I think we should talk before we do. Clear the air." He sighed and rubbed the back of his neck with his hands, buying himself time as he searched for how to proceed.

"This awkwardness. What do I need to do to make it go away? How can I fix things between us?" He finally asked before holding her gaze with pleading in his eyes.

Ellie looked back at him, and he saw compassion and regret lingering between them. She sighed. "Sutton, I'm sorry. It's not up to you to fix it. I'm the one being awkward, and I don't know why. I mean, I know why. It's because we kissed and you said I was beautiful and you cared about me and every other thing that any woman would want to hear from a man like you, but then I rejected you, and I couldn't stop thinking about all of it. Haven't stopped thinking about all of it," Ellie said. Her words tumbled on top of each other while she flailed her hands around to accentuate the message she was conveying. The whole effect was one of spiraling panic, and it was incredibly adorable.

"Calm down, Elle," Sutton said with humor and care in his voice.

"I don't' know that I can," she replied. "I'm afraid that I ruined things between us yesterday. Ruined them in an effort to save them," she said in a thin whisper.

Sutton walked across the kitchen and placed his hands on

her shoulders. She immediately tensed under his touch, and inwardly, he rolled his eyes in frustration that could only be directed towards himself.

"Relax, Elle. I'm not going to kiss you again. Not right now, anyway. I'll make no promises about the future…"

"Sutton…" she said laughing quietly.

"No, listen. I did everything wrong. Every single thing. I said I didn't want you to be my friend anymore, that I wanted more. I'd be lying if I still didn't feel that way, but Ellie, if friendship is all we can have right now or ever, I'll take it. Gladly. You could never ruin things between us."

Ellie looked up at him, hope and doubt mingling in her eyes. "Really?" she asked.

"Really," he replied with a smile he didn't feel.

Ellie's relief was palpable, filling the kitchen with warmth and comfort. She threw her arms around Sutton, her white flag of surrender and care. "I'm so glad, Sutton!"

Sutton returned her embrace, trying and failing to remember that she didn't offer her arms in anything more than friendship. Trying and failing to guard his heart against hers. He was thankful to have the discomfort between them settled, but what of his feelings for her? What of his desire to never let her out of his arms?

He would just have to be content with the way things were for now. Perhaps once everything with Cully had settled down, once he had proven to her that he had changed, that he was capable of staying, that his affections weren't fleeting, her heart might change. Until then, though, friendship would have to be enough.

His heart would have to feast on crumbs.

He followed her as she led the way towards her parent's music room. A baby grand piano stood proudly in the corner near the bay window while two overstuffed armchairs faced it from the other corners of the room. This room was as familiar to him as any room in his own childhood home, and he felt embraced by its memories and comfort. Felt closer to Cully just by standing in it.

"Hello, old friend," he said under his breath.

Ellie heard him and smiled. "It's been too long since you've spent any time here, hasn't it?"

"Far too long," Sutton replied.

They took up the chairs that they always did, and began tuning their instruments.

If he couldn't build a life with Ellie, at least he could weave a song.

Chapter 16

ELLIE STOOD IN HER CHILDHOOD BEDROOM THE next morning, arms full of her bags, once again. She had just gotten home and now was getting ready to leave again. Getting ready to drive back into the Rocky Mountains to say goodbye to her brother.

She knew it was the right thing to do, knew that it was the thing they had to do, but still, she didn't want to. Throughout the disastrous drive from Seattle and even during the day or so at home, it was easy to pretend like this didn't have to happen, easy to avoid the final destination, but now, today, they were finally embarking on the last leg of the journey.

The final goodbye.

"Ellie, can you grab the pillows on our bed?" Ellie's father, Peter, called to her from downstairs.

"Sure, Dad! Coming!"

She retrieved her parent's pillows, adjusting their light but bulky shape between her bags, and descended the curved staircase of her parent's home. They were the same stairs she had descended all her life, marking her coming and going, her every step. They had cradled her as her childish legs bounded down, intent on soccer practice or a trip to the donut shop. Had cushioned her steps as she walked unsteadily in her high heels on her way to prom, had held her feet like a diving board, sending her flying off towards adulthood.

Her father stood at the base of the stairs smiling towards her.

"There's my girl. Thanks, honey!"

"Sure, Dad. Are we ready to go?" She said as she set her bags down.

"Well, I am. Who knows about your mother. Always waiting on that one."

"I'm here, I'm here," Lisa called from behind Ellie, all in a flutter. "Where's Jake?"

"He and Pippa left before dawn. Said they wanted to get to the mountains early so they could do yoga while the sun rises. Hippy nonsense. If you ask me, they're probably going to some dispensary and getting one of those crack cocaine brownies on their way," Peter said with an eye-roll.

"Oh, Dad, I don't know where to start…" Ellie said quietly, trying her best not to laugh. "As I told you before, Yoga is a perfectly normal form of exercise, and it's really good for you. Also, Cocaine is still an illegal drug in Colorado. Jake and Pippa are not eating brownies filled with illegal drugs and they are also not eating brownies filled with Marijuana. They're just exercising outside. It's just like going for a run."

"If you say so, Ellie, but I still think they're up to no good. It just doesn't make any sense. Yoga…" Peter said under his breath.

"Ellie, dear, do you think I should make some of those brownies? Do you think Pippa and Jake would like that?" Lisa said, brows knit with concern. She had missed every part of the conversation except the word "brownies."

"No, mom," Ellie replied. Her mother was the kindest, most selfless woman the world had ever known. In her mind, if her family wanted a sweet that she could provide, it was her duty to provide it. She was also the most naïve woman the world had ever known, and Ellie knew that she would be scandalized if she actually knew what she was asking.

"Well, if those brownies are the type of food you're supposed to eat after doing yogi or whatever it is, I should make some. I'll just find a recipe here," she continued as she pulled out her phone and her glasses. She slid her readers on her nose and began to squint as she clumsily started typing. "I think I read that marijuana has protein in it. That must be why you eat them after this particular exercise. Like a protein shake, dear."

"Lisa, stop! Marijuana is a drug. Do you want to feed our son drug brownies? Get him thrown in prison?" Peter said with a scowl on his face.

Lisa's face went pale. "Oh, heavens, no! Drugs in dessert? Who would ever do such a thing? Do you think I'll be in trouble for searching how to make them? Do you think the government has some sort of tracker on me now?"

Ellie couldn't help it, couldn't hold her laughter in any longer. "No, mom! You won't be in any trouble. Neither would Jake. Marijuana is legal here."

"It's legal? To drug people? Oh, my word…. What has this world come to?" Lisa sat down on the bottom step, lost in thought, phone dangling from her hand.

"You see what happens when people start doing yoga?" Peter said, arms crossed and eyebrows raised. "Now, you've scandalized your mother."

"For the last time, yoga has nothing to do with this. Also, marijuana has been legal here for years. Are you just now learning this?"

"Why do you know so much about this, dear? Are you eating the brownies? Oh my word, do we need to have an intervention?" Lisa was panicking now, worried sick. "First we lost Cully and now we're losing both of our other children to drugs and yoga!"

"Oh Lisa, calm down! Ellie would never do such a thing. She's too sensible," Peter replied. "Now, come on, let's get going. Ellie? You coming?"

Ellie looked over at her hysterical mother and stern father.

She loved them with all of her heart, but somehow she just didn't think that she was up to the task of spending the next few hours in the car with them and their misinformation and overreactions.

"I'm riding with Sutton," she said. "I'll see you there." Even despite the strain between them, Sutton's company was far preferable.

Now she just needed to hope that Sutton would be on board and that Maude could get them there in one piece.

Ellie walked next door, still shaking her head over her parent's panic attack. Jake would love the whole story, would probably leave a trail of brownie crumbs outside of his bedroom door just to scare them.

Sutton was standing in the driveway, loading his bags into Maude's trunk.

"Got room for one more?" Ellie called as she approached.

Sutton turned and smiled, a sight that sent her insides tumbling. His green eyes flashed with delight as he hurried over to grab her bags. "Of course, Ellie! I wanted to ask you to ride with me, but wasn't sure you would want to."

"Well, it was either you and Maude or my parents and a lecture about the evils of yoga and marijuana."

"What?" Sutton asked in confusion.

"Never mind," Ellie said laughing. "Let's just go."

"Alright, but there's just one thing. I promised Rose that I would pick something up on the way, and I'm not sure you'll want to come along."

"I don't mind running an errand on the way," Ellie replied, shrugging as she opened the passenger door of the van.

"It's not just an errand, Elle," Sutton said softly.

Ellie paused at his tone and turned to look him in the eye.

He cleared his throat. "I'm picking up Cully's ashes. Rose

didn't want to. She didn't think she could face it so, I said I would."

Ellie felt the ground shift beneath her feet and felt panic rise up within her. She quickly turned towards her parent's driveway in desperation, but she knew what she would see. Their car was gone, just like the Pierce's. Sutton was the only one left, and now she knew why.

Because he had the unwanted and lonely task of taking what was left of their dear Cully to his final resting place. And now, she did too.

* * *

Ellie walked behind Sutton as they entered the funeral home, the scent of roses and carnations overpowering her nostrils. Thick carpet cradled her feet, and she wondered if it was selected with intentionality. If some kind-hearted soul had realized that anyone walking through these doors would need something soft to land on, something to cradle them as they walked through their worst nightmare.

"Hi," Sutton's deep voice said softly to a woman at a desk in the corner. "We're here to pick up… to take the remains… of Cully Baxter," he said, his voice catching and halting on the hard words.

The lady smiled gently and nodded, offering wordless comfort and understanding.

"I'll be right back, dears. You just have a seat on the couch there while you wait."

Sutton and Ellie did as she said, and sat down. The couch looked to have been upholstered at least thirty years prior, its stiff floral pattern evoking days gone by. Its nostalgia and tradition were oddly comforting, causing Ellie to feel transported back in time.

Perhaps that was the point. Perhaps the funeral home was intentionally dated, a kindly crafted time machine so those who entered could travel back to days and years and trappings that their loved ones may have shared. To the past where the person they lost would always dwell.

Sutton looked down at Ellie, smiling gently. "Are you doing alright, Elle?"

Ellie shrugged one shoulder, unable to say a word. They were waiting for her brother's ashes, a fact that left her speechless.

"Yeah, me too," Sutton said.

"Here we are," Came a voice from around the corner. "You all picked a lovely urn. I'm sure it will look beautiful wherever you put it."

The woman had returned, holding a simple but elegant urn, its clean lines cutting a strong silhouette. Rose had indeed picked something understated and timeless, something that would look lovely anywhere.

Sutton reached out and retrieved it, holding it in between his hands. Ellie had watched those hands all her life, had watched them strum a guitar, type legal briefs, grip and turn a steering wheel.

She had also watched them catch a football that Cully threw, high five Cully, rock climb with Cully, and clap him on the back. Sutton's hands had held Rose's as they danced at her and Cully's wedding. They had handed Cully Rose's wedding ring on that day too.

Sutton's hands had held all the memories and moments of the friendship and brotherhood that he and Cully had shared. Now, they held all that was left of him.

Ellie's heart began to thud loudly in her ears, a drumbeat, a death march. Her pulse picked up speed, stealing any sensation away from the rest of her body. Her fingers tingled with numbness, and her breath grew shallow. That urn in Sutton's hands had stolen every last bit of her composure, every last reserve of control.

"I think I might be sick," Ellie whispered to Sutton as she stood up abruptly.

She ran towards the front of the funeral home, not willing to look back, not willing to see Cully's ashes again.

She pushed open the door and ran towards the hedge that lined the side of the building, arriving just in time to release her stomach's contents behind the bushes. When she had nothing left to surrender, she collapsed in a heap in the grass. Ellie rested her head on her knees, willing her body to stop betraying her, willing herself to find some composure. The grass was soft and cool, refreshing to the touch, and the autumn sun warmed her back.

Ellie lifted her head from her hands, taking deep breaths in and out. Sutton was walking towards her, his hands blessedly free of the urn.

Silently he sat down beside her and draped his arm over her shoulders, pulling her close. Despite her attempts to keep her physical distance from him, she couldn't resist resting her head on his shoulder, drinking in the comfort that it promised.

"Are you past the worst of it?" Sutton asked her tenderly.

She nodded. "Thank you for putting the urn in the van before you came after me."

He nodded and squeezed her shoulders.

"I just couldn't handle seeing it. Seeing Cully like that."

"I know," Sutton told her.

"How can that be all that's left of him?" she whispered.

"It's not," Sutton replied, his deep voice a balm to her anxious heart. "We are what's left of him. All of us and our memories.

Everything he deposited into our lives. That's what's left of him, Ellie."

She lifted her head off of his shoulder and smiled weakly at him. "It's not enough, Sutton. Pieces of him. It's not enough."

He sighed, heavily nodding his agreement. "Sometimes, in life, we just have to settle for things that aren't enough. Sometimes, something is better than nothing, and eventually, that becomes enough."

Ellie nodded as she turned his words over in her mind. He spoke of settling for things, of forcing what was right there in front of you to become enough. As she felt his strong arms around her and sensed the stirring, the desire within her for more of him than she could allow herself to have, she had the feeling that they were both doing more of that than they realized.

Chapter 17

THE CABIN THEY HAD RENTED SAT NESTLED IN A valley on the outskirts of Breckenridge. The late September air had turned the leaves to a vibrant gold, the last flash of color before the blinding and monotonous white of winter.

Sutton pulled Maude into the driveway behind his parent's car. She had gotten them there without issue, a fact that had surprised both him and Ellie. He was thankful. Thankful to share a few peaceful, uninterrupted hours with her.

The awkwardness had eased somewhat. They could at least have a conversation with each other. Sutton had a feeling that the main reason for that, though, was that Ellie's heart was too preoccupied, too distracted with the fact that Cully's ashes rested in the back seat of the van.

"They're here!" Yelled Jake from the rocking chair on the front porch. He hadn't changed out of his work-out clothes—three quarter length sweat pants, a tank top, and bare feet—despite the chill in the air. "Took you long enough."

"We didn't want to push Maude much above sixty-five miles per hour in case she overheated again," Ellie said as she walked up and gave Jake a hug. "Aren't you cold out here?"

"Cold? A brawny mountain man like me? Nah. Sutton looks like you have the bags covered there, I'd hate to interfere with your system."

"So considerate of you, Jake," Sutton said with a laugh and an eye-roll. "Do you know where I should put these?"

"Your mom has the rooms all assigned. She put me and you in

the bedroom off of the kitchen. Ellie and Pippa are in the first room on the right, top of the stairs."

Ellie followed Sutton inside, leaving Jake to lounge a little longer on the porch. The house was stunning. They walked into a large foyer with wide-planked pine floors. Directly ahead lay the comfortable living room, filled with leather couches, armchairs, and a wide stone hearth. There was a staircase just to their right that climbed and cut a ninety-degree angle and, from the sounds and smells that were off to the left, the kitchen lay just beyond their view.

"I can take my bag upstairs, Sutton," Ellie said, reaching for her suitcase.

"I'll get it," Sutton said smiling. "You go say hi to everyone."

Sutton made quick work of dropping Ellie's suitcase and violin in the upstairs bedroom, careful not to disturb Pippa, who was hard at work on her thesis. After a quick hello and kiss on the top of his little sister's head, he left her to it and descended the staircase.

"Sutton, is that you?" his Dad called to him from the back door just off of the living room.

"It's me, Dad."

"Good, I'm glad you're here. Now your mother will finally relax. She didn't trust that hunk of junk would get you two here in one piece." Samuel clapped Sutton on the back.

"It got us here just fine. I wouldn't have driven Ellie in it if I didn't think she would be safe," Sutton said, stretching his arms above his head.

"Quite right, son. Quite right."

"Where is Ellie anyway?" Sutton asked, looking around. He wanted to be with her all the time, and thankfully, he had an excuse. "We need to run through a few more songs before the memorial tomorrow.

"She's in the kitchen helping with lunch."

Sutton followed his father's eyes towards the kitchen. There, he saw Rose, Ellie, his mother, and Mrs. Baxter busily laying out the makings for sandwiches while Peter Baxter sat at the kitchen table reading the newspaper. Rose, slicing a tomato, her graceful silence anchoring the room. His mother barking out orders and laughing boisterously. Mrs. B arranging and rearranging the cookies on the plate, sneaking one to nibble on. And Ellie, standing beside Rose talking quietly while she laid out the meat and cheese. For a moment, it seemed like nothing was different like nothing had changed like they weren't all there for a funeral.

"This is a pretty picture, isn't it?" Came Jake's voice from behind Sutton.

"Yes, son, all these lovely ladies in one spot. It's nice," Mr. Baxter said behind his paper.

"I don't mean the ladies, I mean the food. Meat, cheese, bread, cookies. It's a sight for sore eyes."

"Well, you sure aren't," Sutton's mother said. "No lunch for you until you shower, Jake, and I mean it."

"Yes, Jake, really. Where are your manners?" Lisa scolded.

"Fine, but you better save me some. I'm no picnic when I'm hungry," Jake said as he turned to leave.

"Ellie," Sutton called, coming up behind her and placing his hand on the small of her back. "Mind if I steal you away so we can finish rehearsing for tomorrow?"

Rose Looked over at him, eyes lingering on his hand on Ellie's back. Sutton saw her gaze and quickly dropped his hand, realizing what he had done. It was an intimate gesture, one he shouldn't have taken the liberty to do, but he had without thinking.

Thankfully, Ellie didn't seem to notice. "Sure, Sutton as long as you're all alright without my help," she said to the other ladies.

"Go with Sutton, Elle," Rose said smiling. Her eyes still looked sad and tired but at least she was trying. "It's alright."

Rose looked at Sutton over long then, question in her eyes.

Sutton dropped her gaze before she could discern too much. He had no answers to her questions and would rather not get into the mess that was he and Ellie. He knew by the look in his older sister's eyes though that they would have to eventually.

"We'll leave the food out, come and get it whenever you're ready," Sutton's mother called. "But don't fill up too much. We're going out for dinner and dancing tonight."

"Really? Are you sure you're up for that, Rose?" Ellie said with surprise and concern in her eyes.

Rose nodded without looking up. "It was Jake's idea, and I think it's a good one. Cully would have liked it, and I want to do everything he would have liked this weekend."

* * *

Autumn Darkness fell early, ushering in the evening before any of them had fully realized. It was for the best. None of them were ready for what the night promised to hold. Dancing, laughter, eating, and drinking. Merriment and joy. It all jarred so terribly with why they were there. It was better that it snuck up on them, caught them unaware.

"Why are we doing this, Jake?" Sutton asked as they both gathered their jackets out of their shared bedroom. "Doesn't it seem a little odd?"

"Not really," Jake said with a shrug. "We have to eat. Why not save your mom from cooking?"

"That's not what I mean. I mean, why are we going to a country-western bar and dancing? I don't think Rose is up for it."

"It'll be good for her," Jake assured Sutton, pulling a baseball cap over his shaggy hair.

"I don't think you know what's good for her, Jake. I don't think any of us do," Sutton said with defeated resignation.

Jake sighed and crossed his arms as he turned to Sutton. "You're right, Sutt. I have no idea what Rose needs. No one ever knew her needs like Cully did. Did you ever notice how he knew what she needed before she even asked? Like how he would see her shivering and offer his jacket before she said a word. Or, how he would leave our house to take her on a date always with a granola bar in his pocket because he said she might get hungry. Or how about how he would see tears in her eyes and tickle her before he hugged her close? I always noticed that stuff. I liked that about how he loved her. Cully always knew what Rose needed, and now he's not here." Jake fell silent and hung his head. He pulled his hat off and absently ran his hands through his shaggy hair.

"I don't know for sure what Rose needs. Besides Cully. She needs Cully, and the closest thing I can think of to Cully is joy and fun. This will be fun, and it will bring joy. We'll all take turns holding Rose close, spinning her around the dance floor, and trying our hardest to make her laugh. That's the closest thing I can think of to my big brother right now," Jake's voice cracked, and he cleared his throat, tried to push the emotion out of it. "Just… just let me try and give it to her. Let me try and do what Cully did for her just for tonight, ok?" he added softly.

Sutton pulled Jake into a hug, held him tight, and didn't let go for a long time. "Of course, man. Let's bring her a little bit of Cully tonight."

* * *

The bar was dimly lit and loud, with a long bar along one side and a stage spanning the back wall. A live band stood playing through a song as they walked in. Tables filled the perimeter of the restaurant creating a circle around a large open dance floor. Couples were sprinkled around the middle, some in cowboy boots and hats, others in

Patagonia jackets and sandals, the typical Colorado mountain town mish-mashed attire. Sutton felt peanut shells crack underneath his shoes as they walked to the table.

"It's a buffet," Peter Baxter said as they sat down. "You know what that means, everyone better fill their plates more than once, or you know we're being overcharged. Ellie, Pippa, if you girls can't make it through your second or third helping, you let one of us know so we can fill in for you."

"Good thinking, Dad," Jake said. "These ladies will be needing a man to finish their work for them."

"Oh be quiet, Jake," Pippa said. "You know I beat you during the neighborhood waffle eating contest every single year."

"Well, this here ain't no waffle eatin' contest, little lady. Best leave the men to their work," Jake replied in a southern accent.

Pippa shoved him good-naturedly, and Ellie laughed. She made her way towards a seat at the end, and Sutton made quick work of maneuvering his way beside her.

"Is this seat taken?" He asked as he sat down.

"It is now," Ellie replied with a smile.

Ever since they had shared a moment at the funeral home, Ellie seemed to be determined to find a sense of normalcy between them, to act the way they always had together. He couldn't decide if that was a good sign or a bad one.

Rose sat down directly across from Ellie, and Jake scooted in beside her. Sutton watched Jake next to his sister, amazed by the tenderness that came over his eyes when he talked to Rose. Jake was taking his convictions to bring Rose comfort seriously. More seriously than Sutton had ever seen him take anything in his life, and Sutton wanted to pull him into another hug for it.

"Rose, can I get your plate for you? Would that be ok?" Jake asked gently.

"I'll get it, Jake, but I'd love it if you came with me," Rose said, eyeing him with a smile.

They got up and walked towards the buffet, Jake engaging Rose in quiet conversation along the way. Sutton noticed Ellie watching with tears in her eyes.

"He's doing a good job, isn't he? Being a brother. He's doing exactly what Cully would have wanted him to do," Ellie said with pride in her voice.

"Yeah, he really is. We all are. We aren't letting her face this alone, and that's what he would have wanted," Sutton agreed. "Rose won't be alone. Not for a single minute."

"What about when we have to go back home, though, Sutton? I keep picturing saying goodbye to Rose, and it makes my gut wrench every time. How are we going to leave her at the end of this? How are we going to go back to life as usual?" Ellie asked. Concern laced her brow, and he saw the war that was raging within her.

"Don't worry about that, Ellie. I've got things figured out," Sutton said, standing to go to the buffet.

"What do you mean?" She rose along with him, and they walked towards the tables full of food.

"I mean I'm not going to leave Rose. I'm not going back to Portland," Sutton said with a smile. He hadn't told anyone his plan yet. It felt right that it was Ellie who knew first.

Ellie froze with her plate in hand. "What? You're not? What about your job? Your life there."

"I quit my job." Sutton heaped a double portion of mashed potatoes onto his plate and began eyeing the roast beef.

"But, why?" Ellie asked, plate still empty. "You worked so hard to get that job. It was everything you ever wanted."

Sutton shrugged as he scooped green beans onto his plate. "I thought it was, but really it was just a job. I've spent the last four years chasing after the wrong relationship, the wrong goals, and missed opportunity after opportunity to be with family. I missed noticing you, Ellie. When Cully died, I realized just how awful it is to know that I'll never get that time back. I realized I don't want all of that anymore. I want to be near the people I love."

Ellie stood speechless again, mindlessly trailing him through the buffet line without placing anything on her plate.

"You better start putting some food on that plate of yours or your Dad will be upset," Sutton finally said, nudging her with his elbow.

"Right," Ellie replied mindlessly. She absently scooped a spoonful of beets onto her plate, not even noticing what it was.

Sutton laughed, taking her plate from her. "Ellie, you hate beets. Snap out of it."

She shook her head and blinked. "Sorry, I'm just so surprised. I mean, what did Rose say about this?"

"She doesn't know yet, no one does, and I'd appreciate it if you didn't tell her."

"Of course not, I'll leave that to you," she promised, finally placing some fried chicken on her plate. She grew quiet for a moment, and Sutton wondered what she was thinking, wondered if she was proud of him or ashamed of him.

He didn't have to wonder very long. "Sutton?" she finally said gently as she placed her hand on his arm. Her touch felt warm through his jacket sleeve, and it sent shivers up his arm. "You're doing a good job too. Being a brother. I'm proud of you."

Sutton paused, overwhelmed by Ellie's praise. It was a powerful force, something he wanted to earn over and over again. He looked at her and smiled at the pleasure in her eyes. Sutton followed her gaze out to the dance floor.

Jake was leading Rose onto the floor just as the band dove into a rowdy song, perfectly suited for Jake's purposes. Sutton watched, noting that Jake was no dancer. He was a clown and always had been, but a clown was exactly what Rose needed just then.

As Jake moved in the most embarrassing ways, flails and sways that could hardly be called dancing, Rose laughed and clapped beside him. Jake spun her and dipped her and left her breathless with laughter, and Sutton felt like he was watching a victory lap.

His grieving sister was there on the dance floor laughing. That was enough. That was everything.

Sutton looked down the length of the table, seeing that everyone else felt the same way.

Even Jake's father rolled his eyes at Jake while simultaneously wiping a tear from the corner of one.

"That boy can dance like no one else," Sutton's mother, Janine, said. "I'm going to have to go cut in. Peter, you take Rose. Jakey and I have a date with destiny!"

Janine darted up from the table and shimmied her way out onto the dance floor. "Rose, I'm cutting in!" she shouted. "This is my song!"

Jake turned from Rose, cast a fake fishing line at Janine. She made a big show of biting the fake bate, and then Jake made an even bigger show of reeling her in, acting like she weighed a ton.

Rose doubled over with laughter as her mother joined them on the dance floor. Her father was close behind, ready to take his little girl into his arms. Despite the faster song, he held her close, swaying her to the music, whispering things into her ear.

Rose rested her head on her father's shoulder, closing her eyes in contentment.

Sutton looked away, struck by the tenderness of the moment. Jake had been right. Rose needed to laugh and be held close, needed to remember that she wasn't alone and that joy could still be found.

Sutton turned, ready to ask Ellie to dance, but he found her gone, her dinner plate abandoned. He looked around the crowded restaurant, seeking her perfect frame until his eyes rested upon it. He found her sneaking out the back door, arms wrapped around her middle, head bent in sadness.

He had to go after her.

* * *

Sutton found Ellie leaning against Maude in the parking lot. The doors of the restaurant yawned open, allowing gentle light and muted music to leak out into the crisp night air. It wasn't loud enough to cover Ellie's sobs, though. Wasn't soft enough to cushion the blow of her sadness.

"Ellie, what's wrong?" Sutton asked, jogging over to her.

She startled at the sound of his voice, startled and swiped anxiously at her tears. "Nothing, it's nothing I'm fine," Ellie replied as she turned her face away from his. There was a forced brightness in her tone, and Sutton saw right through it.

"It's not nothing, Ellie. What's wrong?"

"I don't want to talk about it, Sutton. I'm fine, really. You should just go back inside. Dance with Rose," she said. She had pasted on a smile now, but it didn't reach up into her brown eyes.

"I'm not leaving you out here to cry alone in the cold, Ellie. Besides, I wanted to dance with you." He leaned against the van, wondering if she would let him put his arms around her.

"Did you know that Cully taught me to dance?" she said softly. "It was before my junior prom. I was so nervous to go because Jared McIntosh asked me to go with him and I liked him so much."

"That kid from the baseball team?" Sutton said. "You liked him?"

Ellie gave him a look that said she wasn't in the mood for teasing but she kept going. "Cully knew I was nervous so he came home from college the weekend before just to give me dance lessons."

"Sounds like Cully," Sutton said, looking down. "He was a really good dancer. He was a better brother, though."

"He always stepped in like that. If I didn't know how to do something, he always showed me how." She paused and began crying again, soft, silent sobs, and Sutton felt helpless to stop them.

"Sutton, I don't know how to live life without him, and he's not here to show me how. He's not here, and I… I don't know how to live without my big brother."

"Oh, Elle," Sutton said. He finally pulled her into his arms, and she went without protest, allowing her tears to fall against his jacket.

"I'm sorry, Sutton. I'm sorry I'm falling apart in front of you. I didn't want to," She said through her tears.

"It's ok, Ellie. I'm here. I'll hold you as long as you need."

Chapter 18

SUTTON'S SHIRT SMELLED LIKE CLEAN LAUNDRY AS Ellie buried her face in his chest. When his arms came around her, and his warmth enveloped her, she had the distinct feeling of climbing into bed, of nestling under clean, warm sheets. He felt like rest and comfort, and she wanted to stay there in his arms forever.

"Sutton, thank you," she said when her tears were finally spent. "I'm sorry to burden you with all of my emotion."

"Ellie, you aren't a burden to me," He said as he wiped her last tear with the pad of his thumb. "I care about you, remember."

"I do remember you saying that," Ellie replied, laughing through the last of her tears.

"You still don't believe me," Sutton said good-naturedly. "I still have some work to do, then, don't I?"

Ellie didn't reply, didn't trust herself to. The truth was that he was breaking down her defenses faster than she had imagined possible. His tenderness towards her, his patience, his compliments had all begun to work their charm. She wasn't without her reservations, though.

"What can I do, Ellie?" he asked softly. He cradled her face in his hands, and she wondered if he was going to kiss her again. She almost hoped he would.

"I don't know, Sutton. I don't know my own heart right now," she whispered. Soft music drifted towards them through the open door as the band began to play "Like Red On A Rose. " "I do know that I like it when you hold me, though."

"Well, then," he replied softly, pulling her close again. "How about a dance?"

She nodded, laying her head on his chest, listening to his heartbeat. Did it really beat for her? Could she trust what he thought he was feeling even amid the confusion of grief?

Sutton sang the words of the song quietly into her ear, serenading her atop the asphalt underneath the stars. Before she could stop herself, she began to sing the harmony along with him, once again creating a song, a duet between them.

He swayed her and sang to her until the song ended. She felt mesmerized, enchanted, lulled into comfort, and revelry by some kind of magic.

"Sutton," she said, looking up at him.

She saw his eyes flash towards her lips, felt her eyes do the same, and felt herself leaning towards him, desiring to kiss him just one more time. He softly cupped her cheek with his hand and leaned in until there were only inches separating them, centimeters. She closed her eyes, awaiting his kiss but...

"There you two are..." Jake said, sauntering over to them. "What's going on here, huh?" he asked with a sly grin on his face.

Ellie released her hold on Sutton and shot away from him, trying to undo what Jake had seen. "Nothing!" she said. "Nothing is going on here." She put her hands into her pockets and shrugged her shoulders in a comical effort to appear casual and relaxed. Two things she was not at the moment.

"Great timing, Jake," Sutton said as he walked over to Jake and clapped him on the shoulder. "Next time I see you with a beautiful woman, seconds away from kissing her, I'll be sure to saunter on over and ruin it for you."

"An eye for an eye, I suppose, huh, Sutt? Seriously, though, you were going to kiss Ellie? After what happened with Troy? I thought you knew that I punch guys who kiss Ellie," Jake replied, crossing his arms in a sarcastic show of strength.

"No, I punch guys who kiss, Ellie. You laugh at them."

"So I guess this is where I laugh, then?" Jake said, smiling.

"Jake, come on…" Ellie cut in, blushing. "Sutton and I… we're not together or anything."

"You looked pretty together just now," Jake said, wagging his eyebrows at them.

"Well, we're not so, don't go blabbing about this to anyone, ok?" Ellie shot back.

"Not one to kiss and tell. I see," Jake teased.

"Jake," Ellie said, voice threatening.

"Fine, but don't think other people won't notice. You don't share a moment like that without it leaving a mark. You guys are going to look love struck for the next few days, I'd bet. It's only a matter of time."

Jake turned to leave, hands in his pockets. Sutton eyed her and winked before he followed Jake inside. She fell in line behind them, trying not to wonder what might have happened if Jake hadn't walked up when he did.

* * *

Sleep evaded Ellie, hiding from her weary body, leaving her mind to chase after it, to race and run itself ragged.

What was she doing? She had nearly let herself kiss Sutton, nearly let herself get lost in the moment and forget all about the reasons not to.

This is escapist behavior, she chided. You were crying over Cully, something you didn't want to do, so of course, you would want to kiss Sutton. It was a way out of the sadness. You're using him to escape the sadness.

There. She was being honest with herself. She didn't want to grieve, didn't want to cry over Cully, so she was letting herself fall for Sutton instead. It was far easier to get lost in his embrace.

And she knew that's all he was doing too. Of course, he said he wasn't, but she knew better. She knew that he was running scared just like she was. Why else would he try to pursue her now? He had known her all of her life and had never once seemed interested, never once noticed her, never once looked at her with longing like he had over the last few days.

Sutton thought he wanted her, but she knew differently. She knew that he was just sad, looking for a way out of the darkness, and she was the closest thing to a flashlight he could find. They were letting themselves get lost in a phantom, letting their hearts tumble over something that could never be. Ellie knew that once the dust settled, they would realize that they had chased each other for the wrong reasons, and they would regret it. She realized that in their efforts to heal their wounds with each other, they were just carving new ones that would be too difficult to repair.

A heavy sadness settled in around her. It had been threatening for days and had finally won. She had lost her brother and was dangerously close to losing her heart too.

She sighed as she tossed and turned. Pippa slept peacefully in the bed beside hers, and Ellie envied her.

A quick glance at the clock beside her bed revealed that dawn was still an hour away. That she would have to battle the darkness a while longer. Well, there was no use taking it lying down.

Ellie tossed the covers off of herself and quietly got out of bed, careful not to wake Pippa. She pulled on a sweatshirt and tennis shoes and made her way down the stairs, bound for the front door. As she passed through the living room, she saw her violin lying on the couch where she had left it. It's gleaming wood and taught strings beckoned her, but she knew she couldn't play. It would wake the whole house and cause her to feel more guilt than relief.

Besides, it would just make her think about Sutton and how it felt to play with him. How it felt to create beauty with him and then dwell within it, weightless and euphoric. It would only make her feel the loss of what they would never have.

She would have to settle for a walk. That was fine. A walk would be just the thing to clear her mind. Fresh air, solitude, a chance to get away from Sutton and this house, and the lingering realization that it was the day that they would say goodbye to Cully. The lingering realization that it was the day that she would have to say goodbye to her heart for more reasons than one.

She let herself out of the house as quietly as possible, wincing as the heavy oak front door squealed on its hinges. Making her way down the porch steps and out onto the dirt path beyond, Ellie breathed in the early morning air. The sun hadn't yet made Its appearance, but the birds knew it wasn't far behind, knew and heralded it's coming with song.

The breeze, too, announced the newness of the day, and Ellie breathed in deeply of its crisp scent. The chill of it filled her lungs, and Ellie relished how cold it felt, how refreshing and clean.

She walked along the mountain road, kicking up dust and dirt as she went. Pine trees rose around her, their clean and spicy scent filling the morning air. Ellie marveled at how unchanging they were. Winter, spring, summer, fall, there they stood. Their needles straight points. Like a timeline. Never-ending. Holding the moments, the memories of every season. Spearing them, scenting them, catching them simply because they were ever-present.

Why weren't people allowed to be like that? Why weren't people given the gift of standing sturdy and strong, never changing, always present? Why couldn't people be like evergreens?

Ellie felt tears welling in her eyes once more, felt the sadness lodge itself in her throat, so she picked up her pace, walked briskly towards the bend in the road up ahead. She knew she couldn't outrun her sorrow, knew that the day ahead would come no matter what, but it felt good to try.

She began to run.

Ellie stomped the dirt road, trampling upon her grief over Cully and her unwanted longing for Sutton. Her shoes pounded upon the anguish that rose up within her at the sight of Rose's hollow eyes or her mother's frantic glances. She pulled breath into her lungs, allowing it to fill all the empty places, allowing it to saturate her insides and numb all that it found there.

She rounded the corner at a fever pitch, bounding around the bend. She turned eastward, hoping to collide with the sunrise. Instead, she found Maude parked on the side of the road, with Sutton sitting in between the open back door, guitar in hand while he quietly strummed.

Ellie reigned in her stride, stopping suddenly near a patch of wildflowers. Her heart was racing, more from dread at seeing Sutton than from the pace she had been running at. He looked up at her approach and gently smiled as he continued picking at the strings of his guitar. Soft music filled the air, a minor key underpinning the bird song.

"Couldn't sleep either?" he asked her.

Ellie simply shook her head, frozen in place. How could she tell him that he was what had kept her up? That her regret over where they had landed themselves had prevented her mind and heart from finding rest.

He patted the space beside him, inviting her to join him on the floorboards.

"No, thank you, Sutton. I think I'll just start back," Ellie replied, hugging her arms to herself.

Sutton set his guitar down behind him, eyes fixed on Ellie. "What is it, Elle? What's wrong?" he asked pointedly. He knew her too well to miss her angst, had known her too long to beat around the bush.

"I didn't want to find you here," she admitted softly, looking him in the eye.

"Why not?" His gaze held hers, refusing to let her look away.

"Because, I was running away from you, Sutton. Running away from the mistake we almost made again."

"Ellie, why do you see it like that? Why would it be so wrong for us to be together?"

She sighed. "Because we're just using each other as an escape from the pain."

"And what's so wrong with that, Ellie? What's so wrong with letting love ease the pain of grief?" Sutton asked as he crossed his arms and furrowed his brow.

Ellie laughed a humorless laugh and shook her head. "Everything is wrong with it, Sutton! No matter what we do, no matter how deeply we care for each other, how tenderly we hold each other, this ache won't go away. We can't bring Cully back, and sooner or later, you're going to realize that. You're going to realize that you turned to me to heal your pain, and I won't be able to do it. So, you'll tire of me and move on. You'll realize that I'm not everything you want me to be, and then you'll be done with me."

He shook his head and walked towards her, closing the gap between them. When he reached her, he took her face in his hands and held it gently. She saw desperation and sadness in his eyes, and her heart nearly broke in two at the sight.

"Ellie, that's not true! I'm not turning to you to heal my pain,

I'm turning to you because you're the only one I want to feel it with. You're the only person that I trust enough to hold my heart through this mess."

"Sutton, I can't do this. Last night, the dancing and the holding and the falling for you, it was a mistake. I can't let us do this. I can't let us break each other's hearts in an effort to heal them." Ellie gently removed his hands and took a step back. There were only a few feet between them, but it felt like a chasm, one that was uncrossable. She had refused him again, and this time, it felt like it couldn't be undone.

"It's too late, Elle. We've already fallen too hard," he said softly. Tears filled his eyes, tears that she had put there. "You think that we'll get through the funeral today, go back to our normal lives, and we'll realize that this was all wrong. You think that grief has blinded me into thinking I want you. You'll see, though, Elle. You'll see that it's the other way around. We'll get through all of this, and the dust will settle. Then you'll realize that nothing has changed. That I still want you, and you'll still want me." His eyes held so much passion, so much conviction, but it was lanced with pain, and she had to look away or be pierced anew.

"Sutton, you could have any woman you want. Soon enough, you'll remember that and forget all about me. I'd rather we realize that now before anything happens, before anyone gets their heartbroken," Ellie insisted, crossing her arms protectively.

"I would never break your heart, Ellie. It would be a crime to break something as pure and as perfect as your heart."

She laughed dryly and looked away, gazing out at the mountains.

"Heartbreak is a risk in any relationship, Ellie. Why not take that risk with someone you know and trust?"

"That's the very reason I can't take that risk. I know you too well. When you tire of me, it will hurt too much, and it will hurt too many people!" Ellie said firmly.

"Why do you keep assuming that I'll tire of you?" Sutton shot back. Barely masked frustration filled his words, and Ellie desperately wanted to make him understand. He had to understand.

"Because every man I've ever dated has! The only men in my life that are constant are here—my father, my brothers, you, and your dad. That's it and I've already lost one! I can't lose another one. I can't lose you, Sutton and I know if we dated, I would lose you."

Sutton looked dumb-struck, shocked at Ellie's confession of insecurity.

"You have no idea, do you? No idea how incredible you are," he whispered as he scowled at her.

"Ellie," Sutton breathed as he walked towards her. He slipped his hand around her waist and lifted the other to her face. He cradled it there and found her eyes with his. Their brown depths were filled with surprise and pleasure at his touch.

"You are the most remarkable woman I will ever know. You are filled with talent and kindness that most people only dream of possessing a fraction of. And you're beautiful. So beautiful that all I can think about is kissing you."

Sutton paused and let his gaze travel to her lips, the lips he had just barely discovered. He swallowed hard, reigning in his desire, and continued. "If I ever have the privilege of holding your heart, I'll never let it go. I'll cherish you, Ellie and I'm prepared for you to take all the time you need to realize that."

Her eyes flashed, and Sutton saw a million questions, a million hopes, and a million hesitations within them. She wanted to believe him. Her eyes told him so, but the tears within them also told him that she couldn't. Not quite yet.

"No, Sutton. I can't risk losing you. I'm going to go," she finally said quietly.

"Let me drive you," Sutton offered.

"No, I'd rather you kept your distance," Ellie replied evenly. "I need you to keep your distance so that I can let my heart land where it needs to today."

Sutton nodded and backed away, a deep sorrow permeating his features. "Whatever you need, Ellie."

And with that, she turned and ran. Away from Sutton, away from the sunrise, away from any hope of comfort she might have found.

Ellie turned and ran headlong towards the sorrow that awaited her.

Chapter 19

NUMBNESS HAD SET IN. SINCE WATCHING ELLIE WALK away from him a few hours before, morning sunlight alighting on her hair, coating the moment in golden light that betrayed the darkness that it left him in, Sutton couldn't feel a thing. She had left him standing there, reeling, wondering how else he could prove to her that he loved her, wanted her, that she would never disappoint him or leave him looking for anything else. That she was all he was planning on and that nothing else mattered.

She had no idea how incredible she was, had no idea that if he had her as his own, he would never revoke the rights to her heart.

How had he somehow been grouped in her mind with the men she had dated, the ones who left and never came back?

Perhaps it's because you left and didn't come back, A voice in his mind chided. It stung, poured salt in the wound that was already open and bleeding. She couldn't trust him because he had been absent. She didn't know that he would stay because she hadn't seen him stay for so very long.

Sutton knew none of the mess they were both in could be fixed right away. It would take time, and it was time he was willing to take.

He also knew that there were two sides to this coin. Her insecurity and his trustworthiness, and right now, he would start with her. He would make sure she knew that she was beautiful, talented, worthy, and adored.

At that moment, though, Sutton had known when he saw the resignation and confusion in her eyes that the only thing he could do was let her go. That he had to prove his love by forcing himself to stand still and watch her leave. If keeping his distance proved his desire not to, then he would do it. However excruciating it would be.

The day loomed large ahead of him as he buttoned up his shirt and slid his black suit jacket over his broad shoulders. As if the heartache of watching Ellie turn away from him hadn't been enough, they had to bury Cully today.

Goodbye. That's all today had been created for, and Sutton wanted none of it.

Jake dressed silently across the room. Sutton couldn't remember the last time he had seen his friend in a suit. Probably Rose and Cully's wedding a few years earlier. Sutton thought the current suit that Jake was wearing was the same one he had worn that day. A closer look revealed that it was.

Sutton forced himself to look away, to focus on fastening his own cuff links instead of dwelling on Jake's suit. He couldn't let himself think about how a suit could be so versatile as to be worn at a wedding and a funeral. A wedding and a funeral for the same man. He couldn't let himself think about how Jake must be feeling as he fastened his own cuff links, the one's given to him by his brother.

Sutton sighed. "You ready, Jake?"

"No. You?"

"No."

"Well, let's go then," Jake said as he patted Sutton on the shoulder. "Maybe we'll feel better once it's all over."

Sutton nodded, but he knew they wouldn't.

* * *

Rose had found a clearing a short drive up the mountain. Pine trees and aspens surrounded the spot, encircling them in gold and emerald light. They rose in steady lines all around the small patch of grass and wildflowers until, suddenly, they didn't. On the western edge of the clearing, boulders had tumbled and landed, knocking down any trees that had once stood there. At first glance, Sutton thought it a devastating event until he noticed what the felling of the trees had revealed.

The mountains. The trees had fallen to reveal the mountains beyond. Sutton stood staring out at the views while the rest of his family and the Baxter's shuffled around behind him, readying the space for their makeshift memorial. He marveled at the rocky, snow-capped peaks. The boulders had rolled their way down, wreaking havoc and destruction. Pushing out strong, tall, beautiful trees, cutting them down in their prime. In the end, though, the beauty beyond was made visible.

He looked out at the craggy peaks, at the valley below with a stream coursing through it. Sutton gazed at the striking blue sky, at the grasses swaying in the breeze below. The trees had probably been beautiful, but this was marvelous.

Rose walked up next to him and rested her head against his arm. "Do you like it?" she asked softly.

"It's spectacular," Sutton answered as he put his arm around her.

"When I saw the fallen trees with the views beyond, I thought it was just right for a funeral."

Sutton looked down at his sister and saw all that her face held. Sadness, pain, longing, yes, but there, as she looked out on the view in front of them, Sutton saw hope too. Hope that there was beauty just beyond the devastation. Hope that something magnificent lay just beyond the path of destruction.

Sutton held her close. "You know what I missed most about Colorado, besides my family of course?" he said as he kissed the top of Rose's head and then looked back out towards the horizon. "I missed this."

"The mountains?" Rose asked.

"Yeah, but not just how they look. I missed the knowledge

that they're there. You can be anywhere, but as long as you find the mountains, you know which way west is. If you know which way west is, you know which way North or South or East are too, which means you know where you are and where you need to go." Sutton sighed. "What I'm getting at is that I missed knowing where I was and where I was going. I missed that built-in compass. That guiding force. Without these, without home, I lost my way."

They looked out at the mountains beyond them, holding each other close in silence.

"Well, Sutton, you're here now. Where are you going?" Rose finally asked quietly.

"Nowhere," Sutton replied.

"What do you mean?" Rose asked.

"I mean, I'm not leaving. I'm not going back to Portland. I'm staying here with you and the mountains and everyone else. I'm staying so I never forget where I'm going again."

Before Rose could reply, Lisa cut in. "Rose dear, where do you think we should put this table?"

Rose squeezed Sutton's hand, an unspoken promise that they would talk more later, and then walked off across the clearing with her mother in law. Her absence left Sutton bereft, and he turned away from the views towards the preparations behind him.

His gaze landed on Ellie. She was tuning her violin in a folding chair on the makeshift stage they had created by facing all of the chairs in one direction. Her graceful form was draped in a fitted black dress that fell just above her knees. The sleeves were long and loose until they gathered at the wrists. Their ethereal fabric was sheer and delicate, lending her an angelic appearance as her arms gracefully cradled the violin and bow. Sutton sighed, knowing he needed to join her. Longing to and loath to all at once.

Guitar in hand, he walked across the expanse of the clearing, the dirt crunching beneath his black Allen Edmonds.

"Ellie," Sutton said, pulling up a chair next to her. "You look beautiful."

"Thank you, Sutton." She didn't look up. Just kept tuning her violin. Sutton heard the sorrow in her voice. Heard it and felt it within himself.

They sat there without saying a word to each other, simply waiting to begin. A few more friends of Cully's had made the trek up the mountain and found their way to the seats that Sutton's father had set out.

Sutton watched as Rose graciously greeted them all with an embrace, as Lisa walked towards them with a tray of cookies in her hand and tears in her eyes. He saw as Peter, Cully's father stood stoically gazing out at the mountains, hands clasped behind his back. Watched as Jake pulled a flask out of his jacket pocket, took a drink, and then offered one to Pippa. She rolled her eyes at him and then took a generous sip.

Sutton's mother, Janine, walked towards him and Ellie and told them that everyone was ready to begin whenever they were. "We're all set, Janine," Ellie replied. It was the first time she had looked up since Sutton had sat down, and he didn't miss the chance to look at her full-on, to marvel at her features.

Janine nodded and walked to the center of the makeshift stage. She stood there in her black pants suit until everyone quieted down and gave her their full attention.

"Well, everyone, it appears it's time to begin. I'm not one for serious things, and I'm definitely not one for sad things. So I don't really understand why I was chosen to kick things off," she paused and looked at Rose sitting between Lisa and Samuel. Each held one of Rose's hands and had their full attention locked on Janine. "I suppose everyone assumed that even though I loved Cully just as much as all of you, I could get through this part without crying. You know what they say about assuming, though, so..." she fell silent, substituting words with a smile and a sniff, pausing to regain her composure.

Janine took a deep breath and continued. "As I said, I loved Cully. Deeply. Loved him for who he was, for how he loved my daughter, for so many reasons, and I can't believe we have to go on and live without him. I can't believe that I'm here, speaking at his funeral." Janine paused and sighed, taking a sideways glance at the mountain views.

She seemed to gain some peace from the sight and continued. "If there's one thing I am, though, besides hilarious, it's realistic. I can look at things for what they are. I can call a spade a spade and make a joke about it in the process. So here I am, calling a spade a spade. Today is hard. Today is awful. Today is a day that none of us wanted to live, but we must. Cully was one of the best people any of us will ever know, and he deserves our honor. So with that, let's honor him."

Janine looked over at Sutton and Ellie and nodded. It was time to begin.

Sutton and Ellie looked at each other, letting the silence linger for a moment. Rose had asked them to begin like this. To pause and let emptiness ring through the ears and minds and hearts of everyone. She wanted the funeral to start in silence to mark the absence that Cully left. To force everyone to feel it.

And then, she wanted them to cut through it, piercing the void with song.

They took a deep breath and began. Sutton picked out the opening strains of "Blackbird" dropping singular notes into the silence. Dropping tiny clues on the path towards healing.

Ellie lifted her bow and rested it on the strings of her violin, gently playing the melody. She deftly climbed and fell, gracefully adding decrescendos at unexpected places. It displayed her mastery of not only the instrument but of emotion. Every time she allowed the melody to swell and recede, it forced everyone to lean in, to inhale deeply, to feel the bottom fall out. And they all fell with it, if only for a moment.

As the dynamics ebbed and flowed, their audience was pulled in and out, as if riding on the tide. Ellie's bow reached into their hearts, twirled itself around, and pulled sadness out like cotton candy. Soft, fragile, and oddly sweet.

Sutton watched her as she played. Watched as tears fell from her eyes. She jumped up the octave, and he continued to strum. They were building something, and he was lost within it. They all were.

They made their way through the verse again, bringing the song down to a whisper, slowly letting their instruments drop out. And then, their voices began.

Ellie and Sutton ended the song by singing it acapella and their voices blended in haunting harmony. They sang the familiar words, the lyrics about learning to fly, about the dead of night. Sutton knew that by now, everyone felt it. Felt how beauty and pain could fit within the same space.

The song ended and Ellie, opened her eyes as if coming out of a trance. She stood on shaking legs, willing her black heels not to sink too deep into the fresh earth beneath her feet. She knew she would have to clean the mud off of them later. If only the rest of the marks that this day would leave could be so easily cleansed. It was her turn to speak. As she passed Sutton, he grabbed her hand and squeezed it.

Despite how she had put him off, he was true to his word. He was trying to show her how he felt in a million little ways.

Ellie took a deep breath, closed her eyes, and then forced herself to look out at those assembled. Forced herself to hold the gaze of the people that had loved her brother in life, and were loving her family in his death.

"Hi," she began shakily. "For those of you who don't know me,

I'm Ellie, Cully's little sister. I don't really know where to begin here. I'm no good at speeches. Things like this terrify me, but I loved my brother very much so I'll try and be brave."

Ellie paused and looked at her mother sitting next to Rose. Her heart clenched at the sight of them, at how their faces were tear-stained yet they smiled back at her, encouraging her, willing her to spill her heart out.

"I'm not good with words, but music, well I know music. Everything I do is filtered through it because it's one of the only things that helps me make sense of life. So, naturally, I've been trying to use it to make sense of my grief. I've been trying to fit this loss into the language that I understand." Ellie paused, took a breath, and continued.

"A song is considered a singular thing, but that's just not true. No more true than considering a person a singular being is, anyway. I know that sounds odd, but it's really not. A person is the sum of all of their parts. Eyes, nose, ears, mouth. All of that, but even more so, a person is the sum of the parts of those that came before them."

"I am the sum of my mother and father. My grandparents and great grandparents. The sum of their thoughts and actions. The sum of the depths of their hearts. I'm the sum of all that anyone has poured into me, of all that anyone has taken from me. I can't say that I am only my own. I can't say that I am an island. I am a continent. I am a Pangea."

"A song is the same. It's an idea birthed into sound. Embodied by voice and instruments and words. Made real through melody and harmony. A song is how someone felt when they wrote it and how someone felt when they heard it. A song is the moment of its inception plus every moment it's played or heard. It's time unending. An eternal repeat sign."

"A song is the sum of every one of its parts. It belongs to every musician to play it and every person who hears it. It's a nation of sound contained in a few minutes."

Ellie sighed again and glanced out at those in front of her. She felt like she wasn't' making sense, felt like she was losing them, but their faces said no such thing. They were listening. They were waiting so she shook her head, sniffed, and continued.

"What I'm getting at is this. With songs and with people, the sum of all the parts is what makes that thing. Every part is vital, every moment, every musician, every emotion, every contribution. Handel's 'Messiah' would be nothing without the 'Hallelujah Chorus.' 'Stairway to Heaven' is nothing without the guitar solo. If you take away one small part of a song, it ceases to be what it was."

"This is what I've been thinking about since the day that Cully died. I've been wondering what happens to a song when the brightest, most spectacular part is removed. What happens to a person when their brightest, most spectacular part is removed."

"I am who I am because of you all. I am who I am because of Cully. The song that my life plays has always had him as the rhythm section. Constant. Powerful. Beautiful."

"The rhythm section. That's what Cully was for all of us. He held us steady and compelled us to dance all at the same time. He was the heart beating behind everything, and now, he's gone." Ellie's voice caught on the word "gone". She paused, swallowed the lump of tears and, forced herself to continue.

"The thing about rhythm, though, is that it gets inside your head and your heart. You can count it out even when you can't hear it. You can feel it and imitate it even after it dies away."

"A song is not a singular thing, and neither is a person. All that has ever been a part of it lives on within it. Cully is a part of us. I am who I am because of my big brother. He set the tone for who I am through his steady and boisterous and passionate presence, and I think he did the same for all of you."

"I miss him more than I can ever tell you. I miss him so much that it makes me ache but there, in that aching place, there deep in my heart, I find what lingers of him. I find, I feel that rhythm, and it's as present and steady as my heartbeat."

* * *

An hour later, the funeral was finally coming to a close. They had laughed at the stories from Cully's college friends and from Jake. Had cried as Lisa, the woman who had loved Cully the longest, read two Mother's Day cards he had given her—one from when he was eight years old and one from the previous May. They had felt the heavy and aching loss of Rose as she read her vows to Cully one last time, and as she smiled from the depths of her heart when she talked about what a privilege it had been to love him. They had found hope in the words of their family pastor. He painted pictures of Heaven, of God binding up the wounds of the broken-hearted.

Everyone had said something, shared something, given a piece of their hearts back to Cully as they told him goodbye. All that was left was one last song.

Rose had requested that they end the funeral on a hopeful note so Sutton and Ellie had decided to play John Mayer's "The Heart of Life." No violin, just guitar, and their voices, the way they would have sung it with Cully around a campfire. The way they had sang it with Cully around a campfire.

Sutton began playing and then layered in his voice with the beautiful lyrics.

Ellie joined him with the harmony allowing her heart to break and heal along with his. They sang hope into the air, poured it out, offering the only gift they could. That despite the pain, despite the heartache, life was still beautiful. That there was still good to be found.

As they did, Rose stood up with her husband's ashes in hand. She hugged the urn to her chest, and carried it towards the edge of the clearing, towards the trees that had fallen and the mountains beyond. And there, framed by pine trees and aspens and the people that loved her, she opened the lid and surrendered Cully to the horizon. Surrendered him to the view that was just beyond what had been lost.

Chapter 20

ELLIE SAT IN THE LIVING ROOM OF THE GIANT CABIN her family was sharing with the Pierce's. Everyone lounged on chairs, blankets on the floor, the couch ensconced in pajamas and firelight, and each other.

They had finally said goodbye to Cully, and now they were all exhausted. Exhausted yet dreading the solitude of their beds. So, instead, they sat up together well into the evening, playing board games and holding each other close.

"Go fish, madame," Jake said to Janine. Cards were sprawled out on the floor between them as they each sat cross-legged across from each other.

"Don't call me 'madame' Jake," Janine replied without looking up from her cards. "It makes me feel old."

"The truth hurts sometimes," he replied.

"You're goading me, Jake. I see right through your charade. I see your cards too, and you have what I need. Hand it over, you little cheater."

Ellie rolled her eyes at her brother and turned her attention towards Rose. She was next to Ellie, resting her head on her shoulder. "You were beautiful today, Elle. You're words, your music, you. It was all beautiful. Cully would have been so proud of you," Rose said as she pulled a blanket over the two of them.

"It wasn't nearly good enough for him, but it was the best I had," Ellie said, laying her head on Rose's. They had done this all of their lives. Had sat nestled together on the couch, trading stories and love. Sisters in every sense of the word.

"Sutton told me his plan. He told me you know about it too," Rose said softly, so no one else overheard.

Ellie simply nodded, unable to trust herself when it came to speaking about Sutton. She couldn't get the memory of him earlier in the day out of her mind. The way he looked in his perfectly tailored suit. The way his voice sounded as they sang. In her mind's eye, she watched his fingers move across the strings of his guitar, watched as a single tear fell from his eyes as he looked out at his sister. He was too beautiful. Too vulnerable, and she was too.

"I hate to think of him uprooting his life for me," Rose continued. Ellie was grateful. She needed someone to save her from her own thoughts. "He has a whole life he's worked so hard to create in Portland, and he's just abandoning it all now."

Ellie thought for a moment. Yes, Sutton had worked hard to create the life he had in Portland, but if anything had been made clear to her during their trip, it was that that life did not make him happy.

"Rose, I don't think he likes that life he created for himself in Portland. He's not happy there. At least that's how he seemed to me. The farther away from Portland we got, the better he seemed. That can only be because of you and home and, well, this," Ellie said, gesturing to everyone in the room.

Rose furrowed her brow and said, "He said as much to me today. Said that he missed home and family and everything."

"See?" Ellie said, grabbing Rose's hand and squeezing it. "He wants to be here. With you. Actually, Rose, I think he needs it. You should have seen how angry and upset he was at the beginning of our trip. So touchy about Kate and defensive about everything. I mean, he even punched someone. That's not Sutton. He needs to be here with the people that can make him happy."

And he needs to realize that I'm not one of them. She added to herself.

"I'll never turn him away. I need him right now as much as he needs me, but I think there's a problem waiting to be realized," Rose offered on a sigh.

"Well, there are plenty of little problems. I mean, he has to find a job and a place to live, but those things will work themselves out," Ellie countered.

"No," Rose cut in gently. "Another problem. At the end of the day, I'm not who Sutton needs."

Rose raised her hand and put it under Ellie's chin, forcing her to hold her gaze. It was a gesture that was firm yet gentle. Maternal and sisterly all at once. "I know he loves you," she whispered.

Ellie broke eye contact and shook her head. "He doesn't. He just thinks he does because he's sad, and I'm all that's around. Once I leave tomorrow, he'll realize how much better he could do. He'll realize that I'm nothing like the other women he's dated, that I'm not his type and that I'm not enough for him. He doesn't love me, he just wants to be in love, and I can't risk the tension that our inevitable break up would cause."

As if on cue, Sutton walked into the room with a bowl of popcorn in hand. The sight of him made Ellie's stomach flip and plummet, and the tears she had been holding back during her speech to Rose pushed harder at the back of her eyes.

"I think I'm going to go to bed," Ellie mumbled as she pushed the blanket off of her lap. She began to stand up, but Rose clutched her hand and held her gaze one more time.

"Ellie, I know love when I see it. He loves you, and he'll take all the time you need to prove it."

* * *

Ellie roused herself from sleep as her parent's car pulled onto their old, familiar street the next morning. They had left the mountains early so she could make her flight. With Sutton staying in Denver indefinitely, she couldn't count on a ride from him. Not that she felt that riding with him was a good idea anyway.

He and Jake had invited her to join them on the way back from the mountains, but she had declined. Had declined and dug the knife deeper into Sutton's heart. She knew she was hurting him, but it was for the best. Better a little hurt now instead of a deep heartbreak later. No, instead of riding with him, he trailed behind her parent's car, while the rest of the Pierce's brought up the rear. They made a sad caravan, but at least the worst was behind them.

Ellie yawned and stretched, forcing energy into her body for the rest of the day ahead.

"Who's here?" her father's voice questioned from the driver's seat.

"I'm not sure, dear. We don't know anyone with a limo," Lisa said in confusion.

Ellie looked out her window as the car came to a stop, and she saw the object of her parent's questions. A sleek black limo stretched out in front of their house, and the back door cracked open. Ellie knew who it was before she saw and her heart thudded in response.

Trace stepped out of the limo in his perfectly cut jeans and leather shoes. He had another large bouquet of roses in one hand while the other landed casually in his pocket. He looked just as handsome as Ellie remembered, a fact she tried to remind herself of, tried to use to pour some enthusiasm into her heart's response at seeing him.

She got out of the car, ran a hand through her messy ponytail, and looked down at her t-shirt and joggers. She was definitely not dressed to see a man as handsome and famous as Trace Jones, but there was nothing to be done about it now. Ellie was aware that she felt nervous and forced herself to ask why. Was it because Trace gave her butterflies? No. Despite his good looks, undeniable charm, and the excitement of who he was, he didn't. That doesn't mean he won't give you butterflies later. Give it time to develop. She told herself. She wanted logic to prevail, but even still, she couldn't deny the conflict that resided within her heart. Couldn't deny why she was really nervous.

She was nervous because Sutton was there. Watching as another man came to make a claim on her heart. Nervous because he gave her butterflies, but she had denied him anyway and was about to again.

"Trace," she said with a shaky smile. "What are you doing here?"

"Hi Ellie," he said walking towards her and pulling her into a gentle hug. "I hope you don't mind the surprise. You can blame Sarah if you want. It didn't take much persuading from her to pull it off."

Ellie smiled and returned his embrace, still shocked to see him there and more than a little bit aware of Sutton's tall frame approaching. "It's good to see you!" she replied graciously.

Her father cleared his throat from behind her, a stern look on his face. His eyes demanded to know who the man in front of him was. Ellie ended the embrace right away, embarrassed at her forgetfulness.

"Oh, I'm sorry! Mom, Dad, this is Trace Jones. He's, umm, someone from work."

"Mr. and Mrs. Baxter," Trace said extending his hand in a firm handshake. "I'm so sorry for your loss. I can't imagine what you're going through right now."

"Thank you, Trace, you're too kind," Lisa answered while she shook his hand. She couldn't hide the blush in her cheeks as he turned his piercing blue eyes upon her.

"Oh my Gosh! Is that Trace Jones?" Came Pippa's excited voice as she approached. The rest of the group had gotten out of their cars by now. They made their way over, eyes gawking. Sutton stood behind them all, eyes burning with something she couldn't quite identify.

Trace turned towards everyone else. "That's me! You all must be the rest of Ellie's family and neighbors. She's told me about all of you! I'm so sorry for your deep, collective loss. I wish I had words to convey my sympathy."

Everyone mumbled their thanks and then looked at Ellie with questions in their eyes.

"So, Ellie, what's he doing here?" Jake asked bluntly.

Trace laughed and put his arm around Ellie's shoulders, a silent answer to Jake's question. Ellie felt her pulse pick up speed at his touch and, at the same time, turned her eyes upon Sutton for the briefest of seconds. He sighed heavily and looked down, seemingly resigned to what was about to happen. Ellie forced herself to look away from him, forced herself to focus on the fact that a very handsome, very kind, very famous man had appeared on her doorstep.

"Jake, don't be so rude," she finally responded.

"No, Ellie, it's alright. I think it's a fair question. I came to give you these and to offer you a ride home," Trace offered, handing her the bouquet of roses. "It's the least I can do after the week you've had."

"That's very kind of you, Trace. I already booked a flight, though."

"Cancel it," he said, shrugging. "We'll fly on my charter."

Janine wagged her eyebrows at the comment while Pippa murmured, "Oh my gosh," and squealed. Sutton rolled his eyes and began walking back towards Maude, apparently intent on retrieving the bags and escaping.

Ellie watched him leave. He rubbed his hand across his neck, obviously furious. She hated that he was seeing this, but perhaps it was for the best. He hadn't taken her gentle rejections seriously. Maybe he needed something a little more concrete. Maybe he needed to see her with someone else to be shaken out of his false affections.

"That sounds lovely, Trace. Thank you so much for the offer."

At her reply, she heard Sutton slam the van door. Heard his sadness and anger echo through the air.

"Well, if that's the case, you probably aren't on a strict timeline then, dear. Why don't you all come inside for some coffee? That way we can get to know you a little better, Trace," Ellie's mother offered. Pippa and Janine nodded vigorously, unable to hide their girlish excitement. Jake though, simply sighed and looked from Ellie to Sutton, a silent plea for Ellie to reconsider.

"I would like nothing more, Mrs. Baxter! Thank you for the invitation."

Ellie turned away from Jake's disapproving eyes and led Trace inside.

* * *

Sutton sat brooding in the corner chair of the Baxter's living room, a cup of strong coffee in hand. It was bracing, but he wished for something stronger, something that would lull him into a numb stupor instead of invigorating him with caffeine. Something that would pull him into such a state that he would forget what he was living through right now.

Because he certainly didn't want to remember any of it. Not the way that Ellie blushed when Trace looked at her. Not the way he held her hand. Not the way he smiled at her like he knew that he was lucky just to be in her presence. So this was the man that had sent her the flowers. This was the man that had called and texted her throughout the week. This was his competition—a literal rock star. Great.

Everyone had been fawning over Trace Jones for the last hour. The man had been attentive and polite, displaying an unexpected humility and interest in those there. It had sent all the women into a flutter, and both Ellie's and Sutton's father showed quiet respect and approval of the man the longer he sat in the living room. Everyone seemed to like him. Everyone except Sutton. That must have been why Trace made a point of seeking him out, walking casually over to the chair next to Sutton's, and sitting down next to him.

"You're Sutton, right?" Trace asked him, a kind and humble tone lacing his words.

Sutton nodded and took a sip of his coffee, not willing to give the man an inch of friendliness.

"So you're the one that drove Ellie home?"

"I did," Sutton replied evenly.

"Thank you. I'm glad she had you to keep her company."

Sutton nearly laughed into his coffee. The man sat here thanking him for keeping Ellie company. What would he say if he knew that Sutton had kissed her, held her close, dried her tears, and caused a few? Sutton wanted to tell him, wanted to wipe the love-struck look off of the man's face, but he knew it would only upset Ellie so instead he simply said, "I'll always be here for Ellie."

Trace looked at him and nodded slowly, apparently reading everything unspoken that lay behind Sutton's words. "Well, I'm happy to take things from here," Trace said. His mouth held a smile, but his eyes held a challenge. Perhaps the man wasn't as soft as he seemed.

Sutton didn't respond just looked at Trace, hoping his eyes threw the gauntlet he desired. Trace held his gaze, unwavering, and unyielding. The man knew exactly where Sutton stood, knew exactly what was happening. Suddenly he broke the stare, eyes shifting from challenge to tenderness, and Sutton saw why as he followed Trace's gaze.

Ellie was walking towards them, her willowy form approaching with grace and beauty. Sutton's heart squeezed as she stopped by Trace and rested her long, tapered fingers on his shoulder. "Are you ready to go, Trace?"

"I am! Let's go!"

Ellie smiled at Trace and turned towards Sutton with shyness and shame in her eyes that he wished he could erase. "Sutton, I guess I'll see you at Christmas?"

Sutton stood and, before he could stop himself, pulled her into an embrace, held her close, and whispered into her ear, "I love you, Ellie. I'll always love you…"

She pulled away, blinking fast, and he knew she was holding tears at bay.

"I'll see you at Christmas," he said with a forced smile.

And then she walked away, walked away in someone else's arms, and Sutton was left wondering why.

Chapter 21

THE DIN OF TUNING INSTRUMENTS ASSAULTED Ellie's ears as she readied for rehearsals. She had been looking forward to getting back to work but, instead of providing the comfort that she had expected, it only jarred her senses.

She had been back home in Seattle for a week now, but she felt like her heart hadn't caught up to her body. While she was physically there, she wasn't there emotionally. Her heart was in a million different places at once. Part of it, a small excited, girlish part, was with Trace and the incredible weekend he had given her when they returned home from Colorado. He had spared no expense, treating her to a privately catered meal at the house he was renting in the heart of the city. He had been kind and attentive, complimenting her beauty and character at every turn.

He had been the perfect gentleman too. So much so that, when he delivered her and her bags to her front door at the end of the evening, he had only stolen one, soft kiss on her cheek as he promised to call her the next day. She had sighed and smiled as she walked inside, a reaction that only fueled Sarah's demands for a play by play of the evening.

Ellie had been inexplicably light-hearted and happy at that moment, but by the next morning, it had faded. Like light shining on a picture for too long, the colors and hues of the night before had become washed out. Washed out by the reality of the daylight.

No matter how perfect the date had been, it couldn't shake

the sadness that Ellie felt and her sudden longing to be home with the people that shared it with her.

And she couldn't shake the deep desire hidden within her that she had shared that date with the wrong man.

Sarah had sensed the shift in her emotions and had gently tugged the reasons out, pulled them, and then held them close enough to spin them into something comforting and warm. Like yarn from its skein by knitting needles, Sarah pulled Ellie's heart-strings, untangled them, and then wrapped her friend in something soft.

"Ellie, maybe you should have stayed home longer."

"I couldn't stay," Ellie had said on a sigh over her coffee.

"Why not?" Sarah asked incredulously.

Ellie simply shrugged and looked out the window, unwilling to share everything that had happened with Sutton. Unwilling to admit that she was running from him before he could run from her. Unwilling to admit that too much of her heart was in Colorado. With him.

Now, she stared blankly at her sheet music in front of her, focusing her efforts on the language of notes and measures, of key signatures and time signatures. Music was the most transcendent thing she knew. It was governed by irrefutable laws, order, logic yet, it evoked such deep feeling and emotion. It was logical and spiritual all at once. It was ordered and chaotic. Here on the page yet there inside a mind, an ear, a heart, a body.

She sighed, wishing she had the freedom that music had.

The rehearsal began and Ellie dove into it, let herself get lost in the sound. Wishing she could traverse its waves, ride them to a place of beauty where logic and emotion reigned together.

* * *

Ellie sat at her kitchen table later that night, listlessly looking out the kitchen window at the dark park across the street. The leaves had all but fallen, leaving her eyes little to feast on. Her phone buzzed, pulling her attention away from the darkness outside and towards the text message that awaited her. Jake had sent a picture to the group text of him and Sutton on the top of Mt. Evans, one of Colorado's highest peaks, with snow swirling behind them. They were crazy to summit it in late October. It would feel like the dead of winter that high up and Ellie told them as much in the text.

From Jake: "It's not that cold, Ellie. Seattle is making you soft!"

From Lisa: "She's right, Jake. I'm worried you boys are going to get frostbite!"

From Peter: "He won't get frostbite, Lisa. For Pete's sake, let them be men!"

From Pippa: "…Women climb 14ers too, Mr. Baxter!"

From Peter: "You're right dear, no offense meant to the ladies."

From Rose: "None taken, Dad! Way to go, guys. Cully would have been right there by you if he was here."

From Sutton: "I wish he was…"

From Janine: "I wish we were all here together. Too bad Ellie has that yummy new man keeping her in Seattle!"

From Pippa: "If I was dating him, Ellie, I'd never leave! How's that going, by the way?"

Ellie began typing her response but paused midway. Did she want to discuss this with all of them? Was there even anything to discuss? She had only been on one date with Trace, and he hadn't even kissed her goodnight. That was hardly anything to report. Not to mention the fact that Sutton was part of this conversation.

It would be cruel to discuss it with him. Better to be casual and brief. Evasive even.

"There's not much to report. We went on a very nice date, and then he left for the rest of his tour," she typed. "Anyway, I'll be home soon enough for Christmas, and we'll all be together then. Can't wait!"

From Sutton: "Can't wait!"

"What can't Sutton wait for?" Sarah asked, reading over Ellie's shoulder as she walked by with a bowl of cereal in hand. She sat down at the kitchen table across from Ellie, waiting on her answer.

"For me to come home for Christmas," Ellie answered, unbothered by her friends prodding.

Sarah's eyebrows shot up at Ellie's words, and Ellie realized belatedly how they sounded. Like Sutton wanted to see her.

"Well, why is Sutton so excited for you to come home, Ellie? Is there something going on that I need to know about?" Sarah asked with a smile before she spooned a bite of cereal into her mouth.

Ellie didn't' answer, just shrugged as she stood up, intent on finding herself a bowl and spoon as well.

"Ellie, what aren't you telling me? You know we don't do secrets!" Sarah said, her smile growing wider. "Especially when it comes to a man as perfect as Sutton Pierce."

"Perfect, huh?" Ellie said, her back to Sarah as she rummaged in the cupboard.

"Yes, perfect. What happened?"

Ellie sighed, returning to the table. "We kissed."

"You what?" Sarah said, nearly spilling her bowl.

"And he told me he loved me."

"He what?"

Ellie shrugged and took a bite of her cereal, letting Sarah

digest what she had just said. She knew Sarah would understand the gravity of the situation. Sarah would grasp the nuance and the meaning.

"What are you doing going on a date with Trace then?" Sarah finally sputtered. "Sutton is the obvious choice here. I mean, he's gorgeous, hard-working, kind, good. Plus, you've known him your whole life, you're such close friends, your families are close. It's perfect!"

"That's exactly why it isn't perfect. Don't you see, Sarah? When things end, which they inevitably will, it will be so awkward for us and our families."

"So Trace is safer," Sarah said pointedly, eyes narrowed.

"Exactly."

"I don't see how a new relationship with someone like Trace Jones is safer than one that you know you can trust. One where love has already been thrown on the table," Sarah challenged.

"He doesn't love me, Sarah. He just thinks he does because everything is so messy right now. That's why I needed to leave. So he could have some distance and realize that he was just being reactionary. We need time to grieve, to clear our heads. When the dust settles, he'll see more clearly," Ellie explained. She didn't know why, but she needed Sarah to understand what she was thinking, what she was doing. She needed to be validated so she could stop feeling wracked with guilt over the look in Sutton's eyes as she left on Trace's arm.

"Hmm. I don't think you're doing the right thing here, Elle, but I'll support you in whatever you decide."

"I'm doing what's best for everyone. I can't risk our family dynamic being ruined when Sutton gets bored of me."

"And why do you think he'll get bored of you, Ellie?"

"Because that's always how relationships end up for me,"

Ellie said, fighting off sudden tears. "I'm not enough for a man to commit to for some reason."

"That's not true. You just haven't been with the man that's meant to commit to you yet. Maybe that's Sutton."

"And maybe it isn't."

"And how are you going to find out?"

Sarah walked up and rinsed her bowl out before setting it in the dishwasher. She walked over and rubbed Ellie's shoulders. "I'm going to bed. Think about what I said, though. There's nothing wrong with you. You just haven't found the right fit yet. I think it might be because the right fit was Sutton all along. Take your time and grieve, clear your mind but, Ellie, don't let fear and insecurity decide your future."

Chapter 22

SUTTON LOOSENED HIS TIE AS HE OPENED THE front door of Rose's house, letting the relief of coming home flood through him. He had just finished his third interview with a prestigious firm in Denver. They had promised that a formal offer would arrive within the next few business days, but, despite the promising news, he was still relieved to have the interview behind him. It had gone well, but he was exhausted.

"Rose, I'm back," Sutton called, hanging his coat up on the hook by the door.

"We're in here," came Rose's voice from the living room.

Sutton followed it to find his mother sitting on the couch with his sister, a smile on her face. The two women sat clutching each other's hands, trading smiles like the sky trades ends of a sunbeam with the earth.

"What's got you two in such a good mood?" Sutton said, unable to do anything but smile back at them. He hadn't seen Rose grin like that since before Cully died, and it was something he didn't want to end. He wanted to fuel her joy with his own, keep it in perpetual motion forever.

"We had some good news drop into our laps this afternoon, Sutt," his mother said not taking her eyes off of Rose. "Rose?"

Rose turned her eyes towards her brother. They held joy and tears all at once as she took her hand from her mother's and rested it on her stomach. Sutton knew what she was going to say before she said it, and a wave of emotion washed over him. Not now. Not like this. Not without Cully, he thought to himself.

"I'm pregnant, Sutton," Rose said softly, reverently.

Sutton didn't know how to react. He was overjoyed and devastated all at once. Of course, this was good news. Spectacular news. But his sister couldn't be a single mom. How could she raise a child all by herself? How could she look at the face of her baby and see Cully? It would rip her heart out of her chest all over again?

Sutton took a deep breath and forced himself to stay calm, not to panic for his sister's sake. "Are you happy, Rose?" he finally asked.

"Of course I'm happy, Sutton! Aren't you? You're going to be an uncle!"

"Yes, yes I'm so happy to be an Uncle! It's just, this isn't what I wanted for you. A single mother and widow? That's a hard life, Rose," He said gently.

"Any life is a hard life, Sutton," she replied. "I'm thrilled to have Cully's baby. It's one last gift he's given me."

"One last gift he's given all of us," Sutton's mother said.

"How can you be so peaceful about all of this?" Sutton asked in confusion. His frustration was rising by the minute. It wasn't fair that this was happening to his sister. It wasn't' fair that God was asking so much of her. She wasn't strong enough to handle all of it. And he wasn't strong enough to watch her suffer through it.

"Because this is good news, Sutton!" Rose said, scowling at him.

Sutton exhaled sharply. "I know it's good news, Rose. It would have been better news if Cully was here, though."

"He's not here, Sutton! He's gone." Rose said as she stood with tears in her eyes. Her hand was still resting on the flat plane of her stomach and Sutton wondered if she even realized it, if she even knew that she was guarding and guiding her child at that moment. "We get to have a piece of him still, though, and that's enough for me. I need it to be enough for you too."

Enough.

Wasn't that what Ellie had agonized over in the grass at the funeral home? That a little piece of Cully wasn't enough? That she wanted all of him?

What had he said to her at that moment? Sometimes, something is better than nothing, and eventually, that becomes enough.

He looked at his sister, her eyes full of question and hope. "A piece of him…" Sutton said finally pulling her into a hug. "That's more than enough for me."

* * *

Three weeks later, Sutton sat in the waiting room of Rose's OBGYN office, more uncomfortable than he had ever been in his life.

Rose had scheduled her first doctor's appointment during his lunch hour, intent on him coming along.

"I don't want to show up there alone, Sutton. I promise it won't be weird. You don't even have to come into the exam room with me. You can just sit in the waiting room," she had said at the dinner table the day that she called to schedule the appointment.

"Why do you need me there, Rose? It seems kind of… personal. Private," he said, shrugging.

"I need you there in case the worst happens. In case they give me bad news."

"That's not going to happen, Rose. You're young and healthy, and everything with this baby is going to be fine," Sutton replied squeezing her hand across the table.

"Sutton, did you know that the rate of miscarriage is ten to twenty percent?"

"No, but that's not going to happen."

"Did you know that the risk of miscarrying drastically decreases after a heartbeat is found at the first appointment?"

"No, Rose I don't know anything about pregnancy, but those aren't terrible odds. Nothing bad is going to happen."

"Sutton, the odds of me being a widow before I was 35 years old weren't high either, but here we are," Rose answered firmly but quietly.

Sutton stilled, his fork full of pasta freezing halfway to his mouth. She was right and his stomach plummeted at the truth of her words.

"I'm afraid, Sutton. I'm afraid that I'm going to get bad news, and if I do, I don't want to be alone. Please."

Of course, he had agreed, had fallen all over himself to apologize for not being more intuitive, more sensitive. Now weeks later, his stomach was in knots as his sister sat in the exam room down the hall.

Sutton looked around at the women in the room, each sending him a questioning glance.

"Didn't want to go back with your wife, huh?" A lady next to him said. "You'll be missing out on something special you know? Hearing your baby's heartbeat is a once in a lifetime opportunity." There wasn't censure in her words, simply care and warning, but even still, Sutton felt the need to clear his name.

"Oh she's not my wife," he offered with a small laugh.

"Sorry. Girlfriend."

"No, she's my sister. I'm just here for moral support." Sutton picked up a magazine in an effort to end the conversation, but put it down immediately when he read the headline, "You're Breastfeeding Journey"

"If you aren't going to read that breastfeeding article, I'll take it off of your hands," the lady across from him said. Sutton blushed as he handed it to her, trying not to look her in the eye while she discussed nipple creams and breast pumps with the woman next to her.

How long was this going to take?

Another woman who looked like she had reached the last month of her pregnancy smiled at him. "It's kind of you to be here with your sister. A woman shouldn't face pregnancy alone."

"No," Sutton agreed. "She shouldn't. Rose especially. She's already faced enough this year."

The woman's eyes were kind and curious and they possessed a maternal warmth that Sutton knew would be put to good use any day now. "Is she alright? Your sister I mean?" the woman asked gently.

"She is. Mostly," Sutton said, shrugging. "As alright as you can be if you just buried your husband."

Every woman in the waiting room reacted to his words. Some gasped, other's eyes filled with tears, others rested their hand on their hearts as if imagining the pieces breaking like Rose's had.

"That's devastating!" The woman with the magazine said and Sutton nodded in agreement. "I'm sure she's holding on to the promise of her new little one even tighter then."

"We all are," Sutton said. "We're just hoping for good news today."

They all offered their agreement, understanding passing between them. Sutton felt an odd sense of comradery with this maternal brigade and a bit of the unease fell from his shoulders.

Sutton spent the next fifteen minutes making small talk with the women and listening to all they had to say about pregnancy and its blessings and curses. He learned the best cures for morning sickness, that Rose would be extra tired for a while, that a stash of chocolate and crackers would go a long way, and many other little details that might make Rose's life easier.

By the time Rose stepped into the waiting room, Sutton was armed with a wealth of knowledge. He looked at his sister, a pile of papers in her hand and tears sliding down her cheeks. Sutton stood immediately, his heart pumping fast and a question in his eyes.

Rose held his gaze, and then, in one of the best moments that Sutton could remember, a smile broke across her face, and she held out an ultrasound picture.

The whole waiting room exploded in applause.

Chapter 23

ELLIE STARED DUMBFOUNDED AT THE ULTRASOUND picture in the group text and handed the phone to Sarah. They were both in awe and wiped tears from their eyes at the sight of the tiny little life, one that looked remarkably like a gummy bear filling the screen. She couldn't believe it. Rose was pregnant, carrying a piece of Cully for all of them to love forever.

She thought about responding to the text, but the moment was too big for that. She needed to call Rose, to hear the joy in her voice.

Ellie dialed Rose's number and waited for her sister in law's soft voice to fill the line. It wasn't Rose that answered, though. It was Sutton.

"Hey, Elle," his deep voice said. The sound of it sent butterflies into her stomach, giving her an unwelcome reminder of the latent feelings that resided within her.

"Sutton, hi," she finally said, pushing past the surprise. "Is Rose there? I want to hear all about the baby!"

Sarah wagged her eyebrows at the sound of Sutton's name, and Ellie batted her away playfully. Sarah made no secret of her hopes that Ellie would pursue something with Sutton, and this conversation would only add fuel to the fire.

"She's sleeping. She does that a lot these days. I guess that's normal for pregnancy. At least that's what all the other pregnant women in the waiting room at the doctor's office said. I tend to believe them, though, because the paper that the doctor sent home said the same thing," Sutton said casually.

Ellie couldn't stop herself from giggling at Sutton's comment. The thought of him sitting in a waiting room full of pregnant women and gynecological magazines was too funny to resist. "You went to the OB with Rose?" she finally asked.

"Of course! She asked me to so…"

Ellie could imagine Sutton shrugging on the other end of the line as plain as if he was standing right there with her. Her heart melted a little bit at his admission. He was supporting Rose just like he said he would. Upholding her through all of this.

"That was very sweet of you," Ellie finally said. "You're a good guy, Sutton Pierce."

Sutton laughed gently, sending more butterflies into Ellie's stomach. "Not nearly as good as you, Ellie Baxter."

"Sutton…" Ellie said softly.

"How's Trace?" Sutton asked, turning the subject in a pointed direction.

"Umm, fine. Things with Trace are fine."

"Good. I'm glad to hear that he was worth the risk," Sutton said gently. There was no malice, no resentment just gentle kindness in his tone. His words were difficult to hear and, Ellie was sure they were just as difficult for Sutton to say.

She wondered if they were true, though. She had convinced herself that she had made the right choice and distance had certainly made that convincing easier. But now, with Sutton's voice filling her ears, doubt crept in.

"I'll tell Rose you called, Elle," Sutton said, filling the silence.

"Thank you, Sutton," she replied, unable and unwilling to talk about anything else.

"Goodbye, Ellie," Sutton said sadly. "Talk to you soon."

But his voice betrayed the promise of his words. If Ellie was judging his tone correctly, he wouldn't be talking to her anytime soon. Not while she was still seeing someone else. Not while she wasn't willing to let him lay claim to her heart.

* * *

Sarah watched as Ellie hung up the phone with Sutton. She knew her friend like she knew the back of her own hand. Knew her well enough to know how much that conversation had cost her and how much she missed and loved Sutton Pierce.

Sarah also knew the passcode to Ellie's phone, and she intended to make good use of her knowledge.

As soon as Ellie left the table to go and start making dinner, Sarah seized her chance. She typed in the passcode, swiped to Ellie's contacts, and quickly copied Sutton's number into her phone.

If Ellie wasn't going to make things right with him, then she would have to take charge.

"Sutton," she typed out. "This is Sarah, Ellie's roommate, and best friend. We need to talk."

* * *

Sutton sat in his office, looking out towards the Rocky Mountains just beyond the glass panes. He breathed in deeply and exhaled in contentment. It was good to be home. Good to be working again. Good to be near family.

He was happy, for the most part anyway. Happy enough in his new job and new home, but a part of him still ached. The part of him that longed for and missed Ellie.

He had tried to silence it, especially after he had talked to her yesterday. Her offhanded comments about how things with Trace were fine had sliced him to the quick and left him with little hope.

203

That is until Sarah had texted him, and they had scheduled a phone call for today. Now, with only two minutes until the appointed time, worry and hope warred within him. What if the reason Sarah wanted to talk had nothing to do with his romantic interest in Ellie? What if she was calling because Ellie needed some kind of help? She was still grieving, after all. But a part of him still hung on to hope. Still dreamt that Ellie might want things to be different between him, might have decided that he was worth risking her heart on.

His phone rang, and he picked up immediately, anxious to get the conversation underway.

"Sarah? Is everything ok with Ellie?" Sutton said immediately.

"Yes, she's fine. Just heartsick and lovestruck, but I imagine you're feeling the same way since she rejected you," she said casually.

Sutton laughed softly into the phone and he got up to close his office door.

"Hold on, Sarah. If we're going to be talking about this, I need to make sure I have some privacy. Let me close my office door."

"You're office. So you've found a new job? Congratulations!"

"Yeah, it's great so far. It's a smaller firm in Denver, but there are a lot of opportunities, and it seems like there's a quick path towards becoming a partner. Anyway, that's not why you called. What's going on?"

"Right, I'll get to the point since I know you're probably busy. Sutton, Ellie told me everything that happened between the two of you, and for the life of me, I can't understand why she turned you down. It's so obvious to me by the way she talks about you and how unhappy she is that she wants to be with you."

"I'd like to believe you, Sarah, but I just can't. She chose

Trace, not me. Literally. We were both sitting in the same room, and she chose him," Sutton added with a humorless laugh.

"Only because she's scared. She thinks you won't stick around, that you won't stay with her, and she loves you too much to experience that hurt."

"Yeah, I'm not worth the risk. I know. She told me," Sutton said on a sigh.

"But you and I both know that you are. You're already proving your staying power with how you've picked up your life to help Rose. I know Ellie sees it. I know you're opening her eyes to how you stay with those you love."

Hope flared within Sutton. "Ellie said that? She said she's noticed that?"

"Well, no, she hasn't said it, but I saw it in her eyes while she talked to you yesterday."

Sutton sighed. That wasn't enough. Not nearly sufficient evidence of a change of heart.

"I don't know, Sarah. Ellie made her opinions about being with me pretty clear. She rejected me and then left with another man. I don't think it's a good idea for me to press on this. I'd like to salvage what little relationship is left with her if I can."

"Don't you see, Sutton? She didn't choose Trace because she cared more for him. She chose him because she cares less about him. That should make your job of convincing her that you're right for her a whole lot easier," Sarah said with passionate patience.

"So what are you saying, Sarah?" Sutton asked.

"I'm saying, prove her wrong. Show her you're worth the risk!"

"And how am I supposed to do that?" Sutton said in exasperation, but before the question finished leaving his mouth, an answer became clear.

He remembered his promise. The one that he had made while they carted a spare tire through the rain during their ill-fated road trip. The promise he had made before their relationship had unraveled, and she had pushed him away.

"The weekend before Christmas, I'm coming to Seattle to watch you play all of my favorite Christmas songs, and then we'll go home for Christmas together."

"Sarah, could you get me tickets to you and Ellie's performance the weekend before Christmas?" Sutton said excitedly.

"I'll make sure they're the best seats in the house!" Sarah replied and Sutton could hear the smile in her voice across the line.

Sutton would make good on his promise, and in the meantime, he would make sure Ellie would be happy to see him when he did.

Chapter 24

A KNOCK SOUNDED ON ELLIE'S FRONT DOOR, PULLING a smile from her lips like a stitch in fabric, a stitch in time that she was grateful for.

"Coming, Jake!" She said as she pulled open the door and pulled her brother into a hug. She laughed as he picked her up and spun her around, as happy to see her as she was him. She had missed celebrating Thanksgiving with her family. The promise of Jake coming for a visit the week after had sustained her over the small but delicious celebration she and Sarah had hosted for a few work friends.

"I can't believe you made it! I have to admit that I had very little faith in Maude," Ellie said as they went inside and closed the door on the dreary Seattle day.

"Ah come on, Ellie have a little more confidence in the old girl."

"I don't think she deserves my confidence! After a flat tire, breaking down, and an all-around disastrous road trip, I'm justified in my doubts," Ellie replied, laughing.

"She was just having a few bad days. Actually, I think the problem was you and Sutton because she's running perfectly for me."

"I think the solution is not so much you as the work Sutton had done on Maude before he sold her to you. Come on, dinner is ready, and I don't want to wait any longer. Sarah has been working hard on it all day."

Ellie led Jake into their small kitchen and watched his eyes light up at the sight of her friend.

"Sarah, you didn't have to go to so much trouble for me!" Jake said walking up to her and giving her a quick hug.

Sarah blushed uncontrollably at Jake's touch, and Ellie's eyes widened at what she was seeing. Sarah and Jake. Perhaps Jake had been right about his ability to charm her.

Ten minutes later, they were sitting at the table, gorging themselves on Sarah's prime rib. It was perfect, a fact that didn't escape Jake's notice.

"This is spectacular, Sarah. Thank you so much!" Jake said, his usual hint of teasing and insincerity gone.

"It was my pleasure, Jake. I remembered how much you liked this last Christmas so I thought I might as well make it again," Sarah said with a smile that Jake returned.

They held each other's gaze for a second longer than would be considered normal, and Ellie felt the need to fill the silence.

"So, Jake where are you and Maude heading now?" Ellie asked breaking the spell of the moment.

Jake folded his napkin and placed it on the table. "I'll be here for a day or two and then I need to be in California by next week for a few meetings with some investors. Have to keep the suits happy, you know? Then after that, I'm not sure. Probably just home for the holidays."

Ellie nodded her head, unsurprised by her brother's lack of concrete plans. What she was surprised by was his lack of an attempt to hide it from Sarah, though.

"You should come back this way again soon, Jake. We always like having you," Sarah offered gently. Ellie appraised the look on her friend's beautiful face. It was open and honest and filled with hope and admiration. Sarah was interested in Jake and, if Ellie was any friend at all, she would do what she could to fan the flame.

"You know what, I'm pretty tired. I might just head to bed if that's alright with the two of you. Jake, the sofa-bed is all ready to go, and I left a towel by your pillow."

She stood up and kissed her brother on the cheek to offer a

quick goodnight. While she did, she whispered, "She likes you. Don't blow it."

Jake winked at Ellie, leaving her to smile as she walked into her bedroom and closed the door behind her.

* * *

Ellie heard Jake and Sarah laughing in the living room and the sound filled her with mixed emotions. She was happy that they were hitting it off but seeing the blush of new love up close and personal between people she loved so much left her feeling lonely.

She thought about calling Trace, but it didn't appeal to her very much. They usually talked every Wednesday night at 8 because he didn't have shows those evenings. Today was Monday, and oddly, the thought of talking to him didn't cause any kind of excitement within her.

She enjoyed her conversations with him, but they lacked a spark, a connection. He was handsome, gentlemanly, interesting, and talented and turning out to be a wonderful…friend. She sensed he knew it too which is why things hadn't progressed much at all.

Ellie sighed. She would need to try harder in the romance department with him when they talked this week, make sure he knew that she was interested in him. She was interested in him, wasn't she?

Ellie's phone buzzed, signaling a message from the family text.

From Lisa: "Jake, did you make it to Ellie's ok? We've all been worried sick about you driving that terrible van across the country."

Ellie smiled at her mother's concern. "He made it, mom. He can't talk right now, though. He's romancing my roommate Sarah," she typed unable to hold back her grin.

From Janine: "Jake Baxter! You drove to Seattle to spend time with your sister only to turn her into the third wheel in her own home?"

From Ellie: "I'm fine, Janine. I've got plenty to do to keep myself busy."

From Rose: "Ellie, tell Sarah she's a lucky girl!"

From Jake: "I told her."

Ellie rolled her eyes and laughed. Her phone buzzed, and she mindlessly unlocked it to answer, expecting her mother or Rose on the other end.

"Hey," she said through a smile.

"Ellie, it's me. It's good to hear you smiling," Sutton said.

"Sutton! I wasn't expecting you to call," she said, surprised to find that her smile hadn't fallen, but had instead widened at the sound of his voice.

"Well, I couldn't bear the thought of you sitting in your room all alone, so I thought I'd call and see how you're doing."

"I'm fine. How's your new job?" Ellie asked, unable to hide the joy and genuine interest in her voice.

"It's good! I have a great view of the mountains from my office window, and the coffee is good. I can't complain."

Ellie smiled, happy to hear that he was happy. They fell into easy conversation, talking about their daily lives and routines, about Rose's pregnancy and family news. They laughed and shared their world in a way that they hadn't done in a long time. With each word he spoke, Sutton chased her boredom and loneliness away until Ellie realized they had been talking for an hour. Sleepiness began to descend upon her.

She yawned, trying to mask the sounds of her fatigue, but Sutton picked up on it all the same.

"I've kept you too long, Ellie. I'm sorry," he said reluctantly.

"No, you haven't, Sutton. I've loved talking to you. I'm just a little sleepy, that's all."

"Well, you should get some rest then, Elle. I'll let you go," he answered gently.

Ellie didn't want to hang up, but she knew she should. Otherwise, she would fall asleep on the line. "Alright, Sutton. I'm so glad you called, though."

"I am too. I've missed you, Elle," he told her, sending her heart to thudding.

Before she could stop herself, before she could think twice about masking her honesty and feelings, she spoke, offering hope and truth to both of them with her words.

"I've missed you too, Sutton. So much."

* * *

It was eight o'clock on Wednesday night, and Ellie found herself closing her bedroom door in anticipation of Trace's call. She had left Jake and Sarah on the couch, holding hands while they watched a movie.

They seemed smitten, overcome by affection for one another, and Ellie already dreaded Jake's leaving in the morning for Sarah's sake. Somehow she knew they would work things out. It seemed to her that their feelings had staying power, and she was happy for them.

Watching them together over the last few days had only served to solidify her doubts about Trace, though. She didn't feel that excitement, that new blush of affection for him. She simply felt feelings of friendship and it was time to tell him.

She dialed his number, knowing what she needed to do.

"Hi Ellie, how are you?" Trace answered, ever the kind gentleman.

"I'm good, how are you?" she replied, smiling.

They dispensed with the pleasantries, catching up on the events of the last week, and then, a silence fell between them, as if he knew what was coming.

"Trace, I need to talk to you about something," she finally said.

"You can talk to me about anything, Ellie. What is it?"

"It's us," she sighed. "I want to be honest about us. I've loved getting to know you over these last weeks. You've proven to be kind and interesting, and I love talking with you, but I think at the end of the day, we might make better friends than anything else."

There. She had said it. Had delivered the news that had been delivered to her countless times. Unfortunately, it didn't feel any better delivering it than receiving it.

"Wow…" Trace said quietly. "I'm so surprised to hear you say that."

"I'm so sorry, Trace. I don't mean to hurt you and, believe me, I know how ridiculous I am turning down a man like you but…"

"No," Trace cut in. "I'm not surprised for any of those reasons. I'm surprised because I feel the same way, and I was going to tell you so tonight."

"Really?" Ellie replied laughing. "You mean this is actually going to be the easiest break up ever, and we really can just stay friends?"

He laughed too, a sound full of joy and relief. "We really can! As beautiful and charming as you are, Ellie, I just don't think I'm the man for you. I would be honored to be your friend, though. I don't have nearly enough of those in my line of work."

"No one ever has enough friends, Trace," she said gently. "I'm so relieved," Ellie added on a sigh. "After how kind and attentive you were to me through everything with Cully, I couldn't bear the thought of cutting you out of my life."

"I was happy to be there for you, Ellie. I don't know that you really needed me, though. You're strong, and you have a wonderful support system around you."

"I do have a wonderful family," Ellie replied wistfully, missing them all terribly at that moment.

"Not just your family. It's obvious that your neighbors love you too. Especially Sutton," Trace added off-handedly. "I have to admit I wrestled with more than a little bit of jealousy when I met him. When you said he was driving you home, I pictured someone far different. Someone who looked at you far differently."

"Sutton doesn't look at me any differently than anyone else does," Ellie said, denying Trace's assessment even though she knew it was true.

"Sutton looks at you the way you deserve to be looked at, Ellie. I'm just sorry that I couldn't," Trace said through laughter.

"He was grieving just like we all were. If he looked at me in any special way, it was just because we had all been through something terrible together. Raw emotions make for some confusion, and that's probably all you saw," Ellie said, dismissing his claims.

"Maybe, but in my experience, raw emotions don't bring confusion. They usually bring clarity. As your friend Ellie, I'm just saying you shouldn't dismiss all this so easily."

Ellie hung up with Trace, relieved that things had ended so well. She curled up on her bed and sighed, wondering if Trace was right. She eyed her violin, debating on whether or not she wanted to seek clarity and solace in its strings. For once, she didn't. She couldn't push her curiosity out of her mind.

On a whim, she picked up her phone and sent a message to the group text. If anyone could help her find the clarity she needed, it was the people that loved her most.

"I just friend-zoned Trace Jones. I must be crazy, right?" she typed.

From Pippa: "Send him my number!"

From Samuel: "You're not crazy, Ellie. Love will find you when the time is right."

From Janine: "Ignore my husband, Ellie. You're crazy."

From Lisa: "Oh honey, are you ok?"

From Ellie: "I'm fine mom. Not sad in the least."

Ellie stared at the text, painfully aware of Sutton's silence. She had hoped that he would say something, anything to indicate relief or joy at the news that she was once again available. She didn't have to wait long, though. A text message separate from the group appeared from Sutton on her screen.

"Hey, Elle, I'm glad you're doing ok. Call you tomorrow!"

Ellie smiled, holding tight to his promise.

Chapter 25

S UTTON HUNG THE LAST ORNAMENT ON ROSE'S
Christmas tree while she stepped back and admired it.

"Cully always loved Christmas. It was his favorite holiday," she said wistfully. "I've been dreading it because of that, but now that all the decorations are out, I don't feel nearly as sad as I thought I would."

Sutton stepped back and pulled her into a hug as he gazed down at the tiny bump that had begun to round her middle. "Oh yeah? Why is that?" Sutton asked.

"I feel closer to him like his memory is nearer in the things he loved."

"It is. It certainly is," Sutton said, squeezing his sister tighter. He had been concerned that the Holiday season would finally push her past her breaking point, that all of the festivities would sting and rub her spirit raw. Seeing her there, though, glowing by the light of the Christmas tree, his worries were laid to rest. She seemed at peace, and Sutton told her so.

"I am at peace," she replied. "This isn't the road I would have chosen, but it's going to be a good one nonetheless." Rose smiled at Sutton and bent down to pick up a tiny stocking resting on the couch. It looked to be made from red yarn, woven into an intricate and thick knit pattern. At the top, in white thread, the words "Baby Baxter" were embroidered in meticulous stitches.

"Did you see this, Sutt? Ellie sent it yesterday," Rose said, smiling down on it. "She made it for the baby."

"She told me she would be sending it this week. I'm glad it

got here. It's beautiful," Sutton remarked as he took it from Rose's hands. Just like everything else Ellie did, it was beautiful and artistic.

"You two have been talking quite a bit, haven't you?" Rose asked with a knowing look in her eye.

"Every night," Sutton replied casually. He picked up a strand of garland and began to drape it over the mantle like Rose had asked him to, intent on making her Christmas dreams come true.

"Every night for quite a while. I hear you on the phone down the hall," Rose said, eyeing him with a sly smile. "How's that going?"

"How's what going?"

"Things with Ellie."

Sutton hung the last end of the garland as he weighed Rose's question. In his opinion, things had been going perfectly, if not slowly, with Ellie. Over the last month, he had steadily beaten down her defenses. Her hesitance had waned, and in its place, a deep and abiding companionship had blossomed. They spoke on the phone every night without fail, confiding in each other on the days that grief was heavy and celebrating with each other when life seemed good and light. It had been slow and steady progress, little investments into Ellie that Sutton hoped would pay dividends. Little conversations and moments that he hoped proved he wasn't going to leave her or forget her, that he was interested in all of her, forever.

"I think it's going well," he replied to Rose. "She's talking to me so, that's a good thing."

"Good enough to send you out to Seattle this weekend," Rose replied. She grabbed a few poinsettias and tucked them into the garland in an effortless yet lovely way.

"Yes, well, that's a surprise so, I hope she sees it as a good thing."

"Of course she will, Sutton! Any woman would be thrilled to find you on their doorstep!"

Sutton hoped Rose was right. In three days, he would fly to Seattle and put his heart on the line one last time. He just hoped things ended better this time.

* * *

The airport security line was more crowded than usual, but Sutton wasn't surprised. It was the weekend before Christmas, after all. The family in front of him in line had three children, and one was crying incessantly. Sutton didn't mind the noise, but he did feel bad for the little one and tried to pacify him by playing peek a boo when the baby was draped over his mother's shoulder.

His efforts earned him a toothless grin from the baby, one that only served to fuel his excitement at becoming an uncle soon.

Sutton looked around at the holiday decorations at Denver International Airport. Garlands and ribbons graced the walls, and holiday music piped through the speakers. Between the snowflakes falling outside the windows and the holiday buzz in the crowd, the festive atmosphere was hard to miss.

Sutton's phone buzzed in his pocket, and he pulled it out, knowing he had plenty of time for a phone call with how slowly the line was snaking through the turnstiles.

"Hello, Ellie," he answered cheerfully. "What are you up to."

"I'm just on my way to the theatre. We have to be ready for the matinee in two hours, and I wanted to get there with plenty of time to spare. What are you doing?" Ellie asked. Her voice was light and happy. Far happier than it had been a few months earlier, and Sutton wanted to think that he had something to do with that.

"I'm just working," he lied. Sutton hated doing it, but he didn't want to ruin the surprise, not when he had kept it secret for so many weeks, and he was so close to the finish line.

A loud voice boomed over the intercom, announcing that a flight was boarding. It sent Sutton into a panic.

"What was that? It sounds like you're at the airport," Ellie said suspiciously, hopefully.

"No, well, yes I am. I had to meet a client at DIA so we could squeeze in a quick meeting during his layover." Sutton patted himself on the back for thinking so quickly on his feet.

"Oh," Ellie replied. Sutton detected disappointment in her tone, and he wondered why. "I thought maybe… never mind. I won't keep you then, Sutton. If you have a meeting."

"No, Ellie, I'd love to talk. Tell me how you're morning is going," Sutton said, eager to keep her on the line, to hear her voice, to feel close to her.

"No, I'd better go. I'll talk to you later, Sutton," and with that, she hung up.

That was odd, Sutton thought to himself. Ellie had seemed so open with him, so eager to talk and connect. Had he misread her signals?

No, he told himself. She was just distracted by the holiday shows. In only a matter of hours, he would be with her, and he would know for sure where she stood.

* * *

Ellie sat in the green room of the theatre, gazing out at the street lights outside the window. The matinee had gone well, and she only had twenty minutes until the next show. She was tired but grateful to have something to distract her, something to keep her mind off of the disappointment she felt over Sutton.

He had forgotten his promise, had forgotten that he said he

would come to the show the weekend before Christmas. She was kicking herself for getting her hopes up. She hadn't reminded him, after all, hadn't made any kind of indication that she even wanted him to come, but she had hoped.

Had hoped that he would come anyway.

Especially after how far they had come over the last few weeks. They had spoken every day, had shared just about every detail they had to share about their lives. With each passing day, Ellie became more and more convinced of Sutton's affections towards her and of her affections towards him.

Every time he called her, he proved that he wasn't going anywhere and, that had done something inexplicable to her hesitations and fear. Apparently, she had misread things, misread them terribly because he wasn't coming. Not now. Probably not ever.

Ellie sighed and glanced at the clock, immune to the buzz of noise around her. People talked and fiddled with their instruments, munched on snacks, someone was even snoring in the corner. It was the most ordinary performance, and she needed to finally accept that.

"Everyone to the stage, please," Came a voice from the hallway. Ellie picked up her violin and obeyed, shuffling towards the spotlight with everyone else.

She emerged onto the stage with a heavy heart and a pasted on a smile. The audience had come for some holiday cheer, and she was bound and determined to give it to them, even if she didn't feel it herself.

As she took her seat in the very front, she raised her violin to her chin and leveled her gaze at the audience. It was one of her favorite moments of every performance. Her chance to make eye contact with just one person, one single soul. She would commit their face to memory, and then, all throughout the performance, she would play for them. For that face, those eyes, that smile if only to stitch one more thread of human connection into the tapestry of the music she was weaving.

Ellie squinted against the white spotlights, ready to find her person, and she did in spades.

There in the front row wearing a striking suit and a beaming smile, sat Sutton, the one man she had been longing to see.

* * *

To say that Ellie was nervous was an understatement. She hadn't been prepared for the influx of butterflies that would take root in her stomach at the sight of Sutton. The performance was a daze, one that she walked through purely thanks to muscle memory so consumed was she by his nearness.

The end finally came, and Sutton stood, applauding her with pride and love in his eyes. She wanted to rush into his arms, to collapse there and never leave, but she forced herself to leave the stage and walk with a small measure of composure towards him instead of following everyone else back towards the green room.

"Sutton," she said softly, walking to the edge of the steps. He helped her down the steps and swallowed her up in an embrace. "I can't believe you came. I didn't think you would."

"I made a promise to you that I'd be here, Ellie. I wouldn't miss it!"

She looked up into his green eyes. His evergreen eyes. The ones that had been steady and unchanging even when she assumed that they wouldn't be. The eyes that had consistently seen her and cared for her, that had patiently waited for her.

"You were spectacular, Ellie. I was mesmerized watching you," Sutton said. He hadn't let her go, but he slipped one hand free of her waist and cradled her cheek with it. His thumb tenderly caressed her skin and she closed her eyes, moved to tears at his touch. "I'm always mesmerized by you, Ellie."

The buzz of the crowd surrounding them faded, the noise paling in comparison to the thumping of her heart. Her heart that beat for him.

"Sutton…" she said softly. She knew that her tone gave her away, knew that it held too much longing, too much care, and the look in Sutton's eyes as he gazed down at her said that he knew it too.

He didn't look surprised, though. He looked expectant, hopeful, happy. He looked like he wanted to kiss her.

So he did.

There, in the front row with crowds and Christmas music swirling, Sutton leaned down and closed the distance between them, brushing his lips against hers softly, tenderly, reverently. It felt sacred, perfect, right, and, good. It felt like something she could get lost in.

So she did. She got lost in his arms as he deepened the kiss, leaving her with no doubt as to his desires, his love, his claim on her heart, and her claim on his.

Ellie sighed as he pulled away, breaking the kiss far too soon. She wondered why she had wasted so much time doubting him.

"Sutton," she said softly with a grin. "You're a very good kisser."

He laughed, pulling her towards him and kissing the top of her head. "As are you, Ms. Baxter. The best kiss I've ever had."

She leaned in close and let him hold her then, let him prove that his care and adoration would stay.

Epilogue

THE JANUARY MORNING DAWNED CLEAR AND BRIGHT, a miracle that Seattle didn't experience very often. Ellie greeted the sunlight, eager to experience everything the day held. Sutton would be taking her home today. Taking her home for good.

It had only been a month since Christmas had come and gone, but it had been a month full of unexpected changes and emotions in the best way possible. After a perfect Christmas spent at home, Sutton had flown Ellie back to her life in Seattle only to find that she didn't want to be there. Not anymore.

She hadn't wanted to leave the people she loved, him most of all.

"I'll move here then, Ellie," he had said easily. "I just want to be with you wherever that is."

She knew that wasn't right, though. It wasn't what she wanted. Rose. The baby. Her parents. Sutton's parents. She wanted to be near them, wanted to build a life with Sutton around all of them, and she told him so.

"Come home then," he had said as he held her close, persuading her with a sound kiss.

Now, only a few weeks later, she was. She had packed up her life in Seattle and was ready to say goodbye to this chapter, to turn the page to the next. And it really wasn't as hard as she had anticipated since Sarah had done the very same thing.

It had come as a shock to everyone when Jake and Sarah had

eloped on Christmas Eve, but, the two were happier than Ellie had ever seen them, and she couldn't do anything but share in their joy.

"I told you," Jake said, gazing affectionately at his bride when they came home on New Year's Eve. "She's wife material."

The Baxter's and the Pierce's had welcomed the newest family member with open arms, hoping that Sarah would have a positive effect on Jake and get him to settle in one place for a while. Ellie thought that might be a possibility, but not anytime soon, for Jake was true to his word. He and Sarah would be taking Maude and following the butterfly migration as soon as spring came. Chasing down the hope that comes when transformed things take flight. Until then, though Maude would be in the care of her and Sutton, taking them from Seattle to Denver again in one piece. Hopefully.

Ellie heard a car door creak and shut below her window and knew that Sutton had arrived. She glanced around at the empty bedroom, the one that had borne witness to her grief and her joy, and felt only the slightest sense of sadness at leaving it.

`It had been good to her, but what lay ahead would be better. She picked up her purse and walked headlong out the door.

Sutton's tall frame filled her gaze as she stepped outside, and she smiled as he watched her approach. He leaned casually against Maude, his adoring gaze lingering on her as she drew closer.

"Good morning, love," he said as he kissed her and handed her a warm cup of coffee. "Are you ready to go?"

"I'm ready to go with you, but not so sure about taking this old girl along," Ellie said with a smile.

Sutton smiled back at her and opened the rusty passenger door for her. "She'll get us there just fine."

Ellie climbed in, letting the musty scent of old tapestry and gasoline fill her nostrils. It wasn't a good scent, but it was poignant, a perfume that reminded her of the hard days that lay behind them and the hopeful days ahead. Sutton climbed in and grabbed ahold of Ellie's hand, giving it a squeeze before he let go and turned on the ignition.

Ellie turned around to see all of her belongings stacked in neat boxes in the backseat. This ugly, rundown, disappointment of a car held everything she treasured. Her past in the back seat, her present, and her future in the front. It could carry every last thing in its rusty old frame, and despite the occasional detour, she knew deep down, Maude would get them where they needed to go.

It was an unexpected and ugly metaphor for life. Messy, precious, surprising, heartbreaking, joyful life.

Ellie rubbed her hand along the worn, brown seats, breathed in the scent of the dusty curtains behind her, felt the stretched springs beneath her chair, and appreciated the van for the first time. It was ugly, but it was trustworthy. It was steady and dependable in the most unexpected of ways, and, no matter how much they pushed against it, its presence had become constant and comforting. This unexpected, disappointing, messy thing was beautiful. It had carried them through grief and anger and confusion and love and would finally deliver them home. Together.

Author's Note

Friend, thank you so much for taking your time to read this story. I wrote the majority of this book during the COVID 19 Pandemic of 2020. While my family was locked up at home like the rest of the world, this story unfolded. I found pockets of time to write between Zoom chats and helping my kids adjust to online learning. The characters crystallized in my mind and heart as I checked COVID statistics and watched the world turn upside down.

Perhaps that's why many of the themes of this book match the themes of this particular season in human history. The hard themes of grief and loss, of confusion and acceptance.

There were good themes too, though. In this story and our everyday lives. The themes of hope, of relationships, of life after loss, of resiliency, and humor, and yes, love that is stronger than devastation.

I hope that's what we can take away from this. That there can be beauty amid hardships. That even while we grieve, we can laugh, that the people we loved before all of this are still the people we love after. I hope we can take away hope.

I'm praying that you, dear reader, take away hope.

I know no better place to find true hope than in Jesus, the anchor for my soul and the only unchanging, unshakable force of love I know. He has been a constant comfort and a faithful friend since I was a child, and I would be lost without Him. If you don't know Him, you can. His love and His hope are for you too. The good side of bad things is found in His arms.

As always, thank you for reading. I hope you enjoyed your time with these characters as much as I did.

Acknowledgements

It is my firm opinion that nothing worth accomplishing in life is accomplished alone. Books are no different.

Thank you, to the people who never let me pursue this creative dream of mine alone.

Thank you to the incredible editor Jenn Lockwood. You're encouragement and suggestions helped me get this book across the finish line!

Thank you to Christa Holland and Stacey Blake for making this book beautiful. There are no other designers I would rather use!

Thank you to my friends and family! Your encouragement and validation spur me on when I begin to doubt my abilities. I love you all so much!

Thank you to my readers! I hope that you found this book worth your time and emotions.

Thank you to my kids for inspiring me with your love for me and for each other. You three are my dream come true.

And to my husband Scott, thank you for being my cheerleader, the guardian of my ambitions, and the one who knows how to love me best. I love you so much and am so grateful for you!

About The Author

Kelsey Lasher lives with her husband and three children in her home state of Colorado. Her favorite things include spending time with family and friends, podcasts on American History, and the perfect glass of unsweet iced tea. Oh, and she loves books. Like really, really loves books. She is passionate about encouraging people through her writing and speaking. Find out more at kelseylasherauthor.com.